Da
And The Dead
Fish Dilemma

Janey Clarke

First Published in 2023 by Blossom Spring Publishing
Daisy and the Dead Fish Dilemma
Copyright © 2023 Janey Clarke
ISBN 978-1-7392955-0-9
E: admin@blossomspringpublishing.com
W: www.blossomspringpublishing.com
Published in the United Kingdom. All rights reserved under
International Copyright Law.

To Rob my husband, son Iain and his lovely wife Lizzie, my thanks for your encouragement and support with Daisy and her escapades.

CHAPTER ONE

A crash at my letterbox was followed by an avalanche of letters. There was a loud thump, and a sliding noise down the door — ending in a groan. I rushed to my front door, which opened outwards, and shoved my hardest. It didn't budge. On my window seat in seconds, I crawled over to the window throwing it wide open. I craned out of it and saw the postman crumpled in a heap lying against the front door.

I texted Jim my next-door neighbour, *postman collapsed at my front door.* It was only seconds before Jim ran past the window and knelt down by the fallen figure. A long moment passed. Then he stood up,

"Ring for the police and ambulance. He's dead." Jim's words hung on the cold frosty air of a spring morning on Bodmin moor.

Lottie and Flora, my rescue puppies, sat on the window seat beside me, now quiet as if sensing the horror outside in the courtyard.

"Can't we do something? Kiss of life? CPR?" I shouted to Jim.

"No, he's dead and it looks like poison to me," Jim replied.

Lottie and Flora, always sat on the window seat barking furiously. It had been their morning ritual of the postal delivery. The window seat conveniently placed at the front of my lounge, overlooked the Priory courtyard. Every morning the Royal Mail van drove through the archway that enclosed the entrance to the courtyard. The ancient Priory house backed onto the courtyard. The cavernous kitchen, with its stone archways, some dating from Norman times, stared down towards the archway. The stables of the Priory house sat on both sides of the courtyard, and completed the quadrangle. One side had been converted into cottages, into which I had recently moved.

My neighbour, Jim Thompson, a retired civil servant, or possibly spy, lived in the next cottage to mine. He had been living at the Priory for some months. His research into the Knights Templar's and their possible links with Bodmin Moor had led him to the cottage at the Priory.

"It's no good, there's nothing we can do. We must move away from here. It's a possible crime scene. Roy has been murdered, and I think it's strychnine poisoning."

I stuck my head out of the window and called to Jim. "Murdered? Roy Jones murdered? How is that possible? He only delivers the letters and parcels. Why would anybody want to murder him?" My voice sounded high pitched and strange even to me.

***

Roy's body had gone. Shouts and official conversations between the emergency services had dwindled until they had all finally disappeared. Only silence, a macabre brooding silence that hung over the Priory's cobblestoned courtyard. The crime tape fluttered in the breeze, a mute witness to the morning's events.

***

Jim joined me as I walked towards the Priory kitchen. "Yet another dead body Daisy."

I glared at him. "It's not my fault that dead bodies keep appearing…" My voice tailed away. What could I say? My first night at the Priory and I had discovered a murdered woman in my cottage. And there had been the body I discovered when I fell, smashing the cover of a well on one of our midnight snooping excursions to a suspect's cottage. "It's not my fault," I repeated. "They just seem to happen around me ever since I came to the Priory."

"Daisy, perhaps you are a catalyst. A body magnet. Murdered victims are drawn into your vicinity. But this one is definitely a first."

I stood still and stared at Jim suspiciously. What did he mean? And should I ask him? I knew it would be something in a sarcastic vein. "A first?"

Jim stood beside me. His lips twitched and I could tell that he was hiding a smile. Whatever he was going to say he thought it was funny. I was certain that I would not!

"Yes Daisy. This is a first even for you. Now you are having the murder victims delivered to your door!"

CHAPTER TWO

It was without conscious thought that everyone had congregated in the Priory kitchen. We were a mixed bunch of five people who had come to live in Barton Croft Priory on Bodmin Moor. Sheila, a retired octogenarian lived in a refurbished apartment in the Priory house, as did Maggie. Fortyish with curly black hair and a cheerful smile, she was our resident housekeeper. Jim a retired civil servant, tall, white-haired with a charismatic personality, and Martin a former academic who sported a wispy beard and straggly ponytail, lived as did Tenby, a police inspector, alongside me in the other cottages.

Maggie had automatically put the kettle on. A longtime resident of the Priory, she had catered for and looked after the two previous owners, and now had become with us, the new residents of the cottages — a vital part of our lives and a close friend.

"Was it a heart attack?" Maggie asked, turning around from placing mugs on a tray. "I thought those paramedics were not very forthcoming. They seemed to ignore our questions."

"They, and the police officers that came thought the death was suspicious. That's why Inspector Tenby is coming to question us."

"You guessed it was poison Jim, didn't you? That's why you didn't do CPR or the kiss of life on the man. How did you recognize the poison?" I asked him.

"It was unmistakable. Cherry red face, and the smell of bitter almonds are often the outward signs of that poison. I'm not going into it now, let's wait till the autopsy report comes in. But I think it may have been strychnine. There may be other factors that I didn't know about." His answer came slowly, as if he was deliberating on the facts as he remembered them.

"Oh no! Not another murder!" Maggie said.

"Another murder? Who's been murdered? What have I missed? Where's the body?" Sheila had arrived. We explained the death of Roy Jones to her, and she expressed her sorrow for his death. I could see the glint in her eyes, Sheila was excited. This promised to be another foray into investigation, something which Sheila enjoyed. The apprehensive faces around the table showed me that not all of us shared Sheila's enthusiasm.

***

Our statements were given to the efficient policeman who had arrived at the Priory kitchen door. He was grateful for the mug of hot tea, which he drank speedily despite its steaming heat. At our astonished faces he grinned at us, and raised the mug. "Never know if you have time to drink it or not, better get it down quick." He was quite correct, as he had barely brushed the cake crumbs from his jacket when Tenby arrived.

Automatically Maggie handed Tenby a mug of coffee exactly as he liked it. He took it from her with a grateful smile. "Okay Daisy, why did you have to find yet another body for me? Can't you take up another hobby? Perhaps you could try knitting or patchwork? Anything but..." His words petered out as he became abashed at my horrified expression. Tears were not far away from me. I was trying to hold back the shock that I had suffered. It had affected me deeply seeing the postman lying dead in the courtyard. Tenby suddenly realized that he'd gone too far. Even Maggie was glaring at him. "Okay Daisy, sorry. I know you've given a statement, but I'd like to hear it from you now."

Haltingly, somehow the words were difficult at first, then they tumbled out in a rush. I told of the horror I had felt when I had looked out of my window, and saw the body. My words were spoken softly, but still they fell into the quiet solemnity of the others sitting around me. They seemed to echo as I sat at the huge Monk's table, an original that had been in situ since they lived here. Even in the morning, the Priory kitchen held shadows in its corner, despite the modern lighting. The scarlet Aga and shiny lacquered kitchen cupboards in the same shade were vibrantly cheerful in the light of the main kitchen. Large, stone built in ancient times, it had always been the heart of the Priory. It was still. Built on two levels, the kitchen part being on the lower level, archways at the back of the kitchen made from stones of historical value kept that part of the kitchen always in shadow. Jim, our history guy, reckoned that some were ancient Roman stones, mixed with the Norman, and even he hoped Knights Templar stones. The shadows seemed to grow darker. I could almost feel the stones feeding upon the tragedy and evil of the deed.

"It was our postman, wasn't it? Roy Jones?" Sheila asked Tenby. Our resident octogenarian cradled her coffee mug in her knobby, arthritic hands. Bright-eyed, her curiosity was obvious as she leant towards the inspector. The white curls, always permed despite changing fashions, were bouncing in anticipation at another new quest for justice for the murdered man.

A large groan escaped Tenby's lips, and he placed his mug down with a decided thump on the counter. He stared at Sheila as if considering his options. Then his gaze went to Jim, and it was obvious that a decision had been reached. A shrug of his former rugby playing shoulders, a drawing together of his shaggy eyebrows, and he spoke. "Okay you lot. No doubt you are going to get involved, no matter what I say."

Not one of us spoke, we didn't dare breathe. There was no way anyone of us would let an unguarded word now jeopardize whatever agreement we could reach with Tenby. Jim's face was a mask, his eyes upon the pen he was twisting round and round in his hand.

"Okay, it was Roy Jones, and he was murdered. We'll have to wait for the results to be certain, but it looks as if he was poisoned, and recently. I do not want any interference in my work. Any evidence comes to light in your shenanigans, bring it straight to me. No messing about with it. Have you got it? That clear enough?"

Muttered agreement came from all of us. Tenby strode out of the room, leaving a silent group. The moment the door closed behind him there was an eruption of talk. Jim jumped to his feet and left the room abruptly. He returned with a large new notebook. He placed it on the kitchen table and settled himself back in the chair. Opening it, he smoothed out the first clean page, uncapped his fountain pen and wrote the day's date. Silence now filled the kitchen again. Everybody watched as the pen glided across the smooth cream paper. When he'd written the date, he looked up at us. "Well? Let's get started and document our evidence!"

CHAPTER THREE

That evening our meal had been eaten, and we sat in the kitchen, still at the table. Plates had been cleared away and placed in the dishwasher. We sat with coffee cups, and my mug of tea. Jim's notebook had been placed in front of him, and now contained a page of copious notes. From her bag Sheila had produced another notebook, decorated with photos of all the Priory animals. I was delighted Cleo, my tabby rescue cat, had made the front cover. She was in the centre with a border of rosebuds around her. This was Sheila's new Agenda book, large letters proclaimed Agenda, and Avenues to explore, and there was a gap where she had obviously run out of ideas. The conversation now was about the usual plans of action to be embarked on, but as they were discussed, most were rejected.

"This is different. Everyone knows all about Roy Jones. His daily routine, where he lives, and where he goes every day is all common knowledge," said Sheila. I felt certain that her white curls slumped in disappointment.

"Everyone has secrets. Roy Jones will not be an exception. His seemingly open life may well hide a life that has been hidden from view," said Jim. Maggie shook her head at this. It was obvious that she was not prepared to argue with Jim, but her lips pursed, and she began clattering saucepans at the kitchen sink.

A car drove into the courtyard. The squeal of brakes, slamming of car doors, and running footsteps had us straightening up in our chairs, and watching the door.

"You have to help us! She's been wrongly accused, Mary didn't do it!" Demelza raced into the kitchen, banging the door back violently against a kitchen cupboard. She pulled a small woman through the open doorway into the kitchen. "This is Mary Jones, she's Roy's wife and the police think she's killed him. We think they are going to arrest her for his murder."

The woman stood in front of us, her head was bowed down, and she shuffled her feet nervously. A beige colour was what I immediately thought of. She had pale brown washed out eyes, which were echoed in the faded brown hair. Her brown trousers were worn with a fawn jacket, and porridge coloured sweater. We stared at her, not one of us knew what to say. Finally, she looked up at us all, and spoke. "Demelza says you can help me. I didn't kill him. The police asked me the same questions again and again. I didn't see him last night. I was at the church hall, it was my line dancing class. When I got back, I found a note from Roy saying he was taking off for a while. He needed a break from routine, and he would phone me soon to let me know where he was."

The words were said in a flat monotone. If sound could have a colour, those words would also be beige. At the end of this speech her voice rose slightly, with tension creeping into it. I saw that her hands had tightened almost into fists. A deep breath, and she continued speaking. "I wanted a divorce. It wasn't common knowledge, but I had seen my solicitor. Roy had been having affairs. I don't know who they were, but he'd been seen in Bodmin with various women. I don't think I really wanted to know. But I knew I could not live like this anymore, so I began to find out about a divorce. The police have found this out, and they think I took a shortcut and murdered him!"

"Why didn't you pack a bag and leave?" Sheila's abrupt question made Mary turn angrily towards her.

"It's my house! I inherited it from my grandmother, and he wouldn't leave. He wasn't abusive so I couldn't get a restraining order. I didn't know how to get him out of my house, and he knew it. And we had a row about it..." Mary took a deep breath and suddenly sat down in the chair, her head in her hands.

"What Mary is trying to tell you is that she did have a huge row with Roy. And that row was in the community shop, where normally quiet Mary suddenly shouted at him and..."

"What Demelza is about to tell you is that I... I swore I'd kill him if he didn't leave my house! But I didn't kill him, I couldn't kill anyone," Mary cried out in despair.

"Now you see why she's the number one suspect! She's innocent. Mary wouldn't kill anyone, and you lot have got to find out who the killer is and clear Mary's name." Demelza had been pacing up and down the kitchen in her agitation, but suddenly she came forward and pointed to me. "You have to clear her name Daisy! She's a distant cousin of ours, she's family. And family stick together, don't we?"

What could I say? Family? Was I related to this mouselike woman? A small voice in my head murmured, are you any different to her? Wasn't I like her? Perhaps not quite as mousy, but I stayed in a marriage for far too long, with someone I didn't like, let alone love. Should it make any difference that she was a cousin, however distant? I was new to this *family* business, having been told when adopted, that I was the last of my family.

Maggie brought mugs of coffee over for Mary and Demelza, and patted Mary on the back. "We'll help you. If you were guilty, you wouldn't come to us to ask us to solve the murder."

"Of course, she wouldn't," Sheila declared and gave Mary an encouraging smile. An exchange of glances between Jim and myself, showed me that not only had I become cynical like Jim, but we were often on the same wavelength. It could have been a double bluff was my immediate thought, and I knew it had also been Jim's.

Sheila's Agenda book was flourished, and she reached for her pen. Jim's notebook which had been on the kitchen dresser, was lifted off and handed to Jim by Maggie with a hopeful look.

***

Sometime later Demelza took Mary home. Sheila demanded of Jim in a quiet fury. "That was a cross-examination you put that poor woman through. You would have thought you were in 'Gitmo' interrogating her like that!"

"Gitmo?" A puzzled Martin asked Sheila.

"Guantánamo Bay of course! The prison in Cuba where all the American terrorist prisoners arc sent," Sheila snapped in a quick aside to him.

Maggie's eyes rolled in her head, Jim shook his head, but I just grinned. Sheila loved using American cop TV show words and introduced a new word at intervals. Some were better than others, "hauling her butt," had been a popular phrase lately. I disliked that one.

"I was getting all the facts Sheila. I was only questioning her just as the police will be doing in the next few days. They will ask harsher questions than those I asked her. It wouldn't have helped her if I had been too nice when asking her difficult questions," was Jim's answer. He concentrated on his fountain pen, replacing the top carefully, and putting it straight beside the notebook.

"Okay," Sheila subsided, her eyes still doubtful as they focused on him.

"She's not telling you everything," said Maggie.

"I realize that. What was she hiding? Do you know

Maggie?" Jim asked.

Maggie shook her head, "I don't know. I've known Mary for some time. I think she was hiding something, but I don't know what it was."

"She couldn't leave, it was her own house. That poor woman. We must help her," exclaimed Sheila.

"We were going to investigate this murder anyway. Having this request from Mary just gives us a personal focus. Yes Sheila, we will try to find out why Roy Jones was murdered." Jim said solemnly as he looked at the octogenarian. Sheila nodded her head, if Jim said he was doing something, to Sheila that was as good as a promise. "And we will find out who murdered him!"

CHAPTER FOUR

The rain grew heavier next morning. "What a horrible day," I told my pets, or the 'guys' as I had named them. Calling the three names, Cleo, Lottie and Flora, one after the other was time-consuming and sounded silly. Yelling 'guys' was more efficient and easier, and to my delight they understood it meant them. "Coffee time at the Priory for me. If it ever stops raining, I'll get you out for a walk when I get back," I promised them. Popping into the Priory kitchen for morning coffee, meant I could catch up on any gossip. In my case it was always a mug of tea, coffee didn't like me. I hoped Maggie had made some of her fantastic chocolate chip cookies. I promised myself that I would eat only one. I knew that I had lied to myself, I could never stop at just one.

***

Settled around the table in the kitchen, Jim, Martin, and I moaned about the weather. But it was Sheila who marched in angrily. "It's dreadful. It's so bad I can't get out on my scooter. Too wet!" She slumped into a chair. "Anybody got any news?" A short time ago Sheila bought a new mobility scooter with huge tyres, and able to go over most of the rough land around the Priory. It had been a great delight for her to travel around the rough tracks and fields with her grandchildren. That mobility scooter had played a vital part in our last escapade, during which we rescued the puppies from the cruel puppy farmer and his murdering associate.

"Nothing," said Martin. His face and beard straggled in dejection at the dreadful weather and the lack of news. Shy and unassuming Martin had become a millionaire at the beginning of the bitcoin episode. He had bought the Priory from the previous owner, who, distressed at the murders fled to America for a quieter life in academia. Martin still lived in one of the cottages where he moved to originally. The Priory House itself had been converted into flats, Maggie and Sheila each lived in one. The larger flat still remained empty, Martin preferred to live in his cottage, he didn't fancy the grand apartment.

"How do we get news about Roy? It's not as if he went to the hairdressers," grumbled Sheila as she cupped her mug of coffee in her hands.

"No, but Mary his wife does. Could you get any gossip if you went to the hairdressers Sheila?" I suggested. "We've met Mary, but additional information on her would be good."

A nod of approval from Jim greeted this remark.

Sheila perked up. "I can't go out on my scooter so I might as well go and get some information at the hairdressers, and I'd love to get my hair done. I wonder if they have a cancellation?" They did, but could she be there at the hairdressers in fifteen minutes? Sheila said she could. She raced from the kitchen, actually she hobbled quickly, all grumbles forgotten.

Demelza had joined us. "I called on Mary this morning. She's withdrawn completely, and wouldn't even let me in the house, so I thought it best to leave her and join you for coffee." Leaning against the counter she waited for the second pot of coffee to brew. That was unusual for Demelza. She never dropped in for coffee, and she looked tired with dark shadows beneath her eyes. I was worried about Demelza, she had been looking preoccupied for some time. Her normally cheerful personality had been subdued and even fearful. Later, I promised myself that I would get her alone and try to find out what exactly was the problem.

The door opened, and Gerald came in. "Can we join you for coffee?" A large burly figure followed him. I drew in my breath. I would recognize that hulk of a man anywhere. Jim was sitting next to me. He heard that sharp intake of breath I made, and reached under the table to grab my hand and give it a squeeze. "This is my older brother Sam," Gerald's voice was harsh with tension. Some time ago Sam had shot and wounded Jim, and terrified me. He had been under the misapprehension that there had been a hidden treasure in the Priory, and that Jim was deliberately thwarting Gerald's efforts at legitimate research on the Knights Templars. It had always seemed to me that he had read and swallowed the Da Vinci Code whole, and believed every word of it. Now he wished to return to Cornwall and live in the village beside us! A recent stint in Spain had left him unhappy and miserable, missing both Cornwall and his brother. He had promised that he had turned over a new leaf and was going straight. I had agreed, but still hadn't worked out my emotional reaction to him. I stared at him, said nothing, but reached for the knife on the table. It was a large one that Maggie had used to cut the coffee cream cake that she had produced at coffee time. It was good, but I still preferred her chocolate chip cookies.

Sam's face was new to me, but the eyes had been clearly seen above the balaclava he had worn. Those eyes looked straight at me now. No longer did they hold anger and evil intent. To my discomfiture they were laughing! That smiley mouth, firm chin with a dimple in it were a revelation. "You won't need the knife Daisy. I come in peace and I'm without any weapons," Sam said.

Embarrassed as all eyes fell upon my white knuckled hand holding the knife, I dropped it and left it on the table. I muttered a greeting. Sam acknowledged each member of the group and finally turned towards

Demelza. I had never believed in it. To be honest I thought it a myth. But, before each of our eyes we saw it occur. Sam stared at Demelza as she poured coffee refills for us, and new coffee mugs for herself, Sam, and Gerald. When Demelza turned round mugs in hand, she looked at Sam. Demelza and Sam stared at each other and in that instant, everyone watching knew that they had fallen in love. Was it for seconds? Or was it minutes? The kitchen itself seemed to hold still for that to happen. Love at first sight, and they were both speechless. We all knew it had happened, and had seen it in action ourselves.

Normal conversation resumed, and Sam and Gerald joined us at the table. All our talk was about the murder of the postman. Demelza had sat opposite Sam, and it was amusing to watch the sly, getting to know you looks passing between them. My fear of Sam vanished as I watched him become smitten by Demelza. But and it was a big but, I was still wary of him. For Gerald's sake I would make the effort to be pleasant to him. However, I would always be on my guard with him.

"Lunch at the pub anyone?" Jim looked around the table. "There may be a few people there eager to chat about the murder. I'm sure it will be the main topic of conversation. We may well hear something of value."

"The hairdressers and now the pub. What else? Where next can we investigate?" Martin asked us. "But we must only investigate stuff that Tenby won't mind us looking into."

"Arthur! He's the old man who lives in one of the cottages down by the river. He retired a couple of years ago, but he was a postman and worked with Roy before retirement. He might be able to give us more information, he must have known Roy well," Demelza said.

"Demelza, do you know if he would mind us calling in for a chat?" Jim asked.

"He will be only too happy to help. He was a great friend of my dad and Mary's father. He'll do anything to help us prove Mary's innocence," Demelza said.

"That's the pub, the hairdresser and Arthur. Surely we'll get some information from that lot," said Jim. He put his cap on his fountain pen, and stood up. "Let's go!"

CHAPTER FIVE

The Red Lion pub was crowded. It was almost spring, but it was not tourists who had felt the urgent need for a pint and lunch. Not this morning. It was locals who had wandered in hopeful of finding out what exactly had happened at the Priory courtyard. Dogs are always welcome at the Red Lion pub. A large jar of doggy treats sat on the bar ready for every dog who entered. Our three dogs had never been before, so bringing them was a new experience for them. A new experience for us too! Martin had Flora on the lead, I carried Lottie in my arms, and Maisie followed Maggie into the pub with gentle coaxing. The outgoing Flora with her adoration of all men, loved Martin since he had become her puppy training guy. I had fought hard against taking on any more pets. But both Cleo and Flora had become friends with Lottie when she arrived as a rescue puppy. I hadn't wanted to take on Lottie, feeling that with a cat and a dog, I had enough to look after. But Lottie had proved to be a gallant little dog helping Sheila and I in our earlier adventures. I accepted that Lottie was going to be my third pet. Surprisingly, Lottie never held my initial refusal to add her to my household against me. Her devotion to me was overwhelming. She had become my shadow giving me an intense love.

We sat at a round table that was centrally placed in the pub. A large log fire crackled giving out a welcome warmth after the cold wind and sleety rain outside. Spring was late this year, and Bodmin Moor still felt in the grip of winter. I sat down and inhaled the pub aromas that wafted around us. It was comprised of wood smoke, chips, and the earthy smell of hoppy real ales. It was a comforting fug, and I felt my limbs begin to relax. The voices at the next table drifted over towards us. Their chat was about the murder. Maggie and I strained towards the voices, eager to hear anything that might be of use in our investigations.

"It was that Roy Jones that they found. Poisoned he was." A woman dressed in well-worn waterproof jacket said authoritatively to the other two seated at her table. A large man sat beside her, the glass of beer in his hand was half full. Three other empty glasses stood in front of him. The other person at the table was a woman I had seen in the community shop previously. She was hard to miss, having a flamboyant reddish haircut, with enormous glasses through which she glared around the room.

"Always knew that he'd come to a sticky end, that Mary was a saint to put up with his escapades. Late nights and staying weekends in Bodmin town. We all knew what he was getting up to!" The waterproof jacket lady continued speaking. "Women! Constant procession of them, he was always after them. That poor wife of his!"

Nods of agreement, and murmured assent greeted her remarks.

When Martin and Jim arrived back with the drinks, we gestured them into silence, indicating conversation at the next table. They sat down, gave us our drinks and both leaned to the side. I had to smile, we were all leaning towards that table, trying not to miss anything in their conversation. It looked as if we were all in a stiff breeze!

"That cottage they live in belonged to her grandma. She couldn't walk out and leave that behind," said the red haired woman, downing a large gin and proffering her empty glass towards the man. He quickly drained his pint, looked round at the waterproof jacket lady who nodded, and he went up for yet another round of drinks. "Mary knew what he was up to. She wasn't a fool. But what could she do? I know she tried to throw him out, but he wasn't abusive towards her. Mary was always a shy little thing, letting him get away with it time after time. She couldn't bear confrontation and didn't stand up for herself. But I'd have changed the locks on him!" She tapped the waterproof jacket lady on the arm. "The police think she did it. They were in her cottage talking for a long time. It's a matter of finding the right evidence and then they will convict her. Didn't think much of that Roy myself, too nosy. Some of my letters looked as if they'd been steamed open when I got them. I don't have anything to hide, he could read whatever he wanted in my post. Not sure that applies to everyone in this village. Maybe he found out something that was too dangerous for him to know!"

Maggie gave a gasp and put her hand over her mouth. Her horrified expression said it all. It was obvious from this conversation that everyone thought Mary had done it. The general consensus of opinion was surprise that Mary hadn't killed him before. But what did the red haired woman mean about him finding out dangerous secrets. I saw this was a new idea to all of us, and Jim assumed a thoughtful look as he drank his beer and listened intently. Unfortunately, we got no more information. When the beer drinker resumed his seat, conversation turned towards the weather.

"I don't believe that Mary killed him. I grew up with Mary. I went to school with her and she very rarely loses her temper. Surely she wouldn't have…" Maggie's voice drifted off into a silence pregnant with meaning.

"I don't discount the possibility that Mary could have killed her husband. It was obvious that she had reasons enough to murder him. But where would she get that poison? And did she hate him enough to actually do it?" Jim said.

"When did she do it? How long would the poison take to act?" Martin asked Jim.

"You're right Martin. If we try and work out the time the poison was given, we can find out who actually has an alibi for that time," said Jim.

"What was that all about, Roy steaming open envelopes, and having a dangerous secret?" I asked.

"That's another avenue for us to explore. This is new information about the possibility of him having dangerous secrets. Could he be a blackmailer?" Jim said.

The conversations around us held no further information and were just general chitchat. We had ordered a Ploughman's lunch for us all. Somehow, we managed to eat it. But it was difficult because the dogs began to act up. Flora was bored, and she started fidgeting, setting off Maisie and Lottie. Trying to get them to sit whilst we ate our meals became increasingly difficult. Flora wanted to greet every man in the room. Maisie thought she would follow Flora.

"Next time we bring them down, we only have a drink!" I said rising to my feet to leave the pub. A text came through from Violet. I had not realized that I had a twin sister until I moved to Cornwall armed with a newly discovered photograph with cryptic clues to my family heritage. Following the clues from the photograph, I discovered not only a twin sister, but my mother. In her nineties she lived in a care home near St Austell. Alert and fully aware of this momentous discovery to all of us, she had welcomed me eventually, into the family. My son Jake resembled her dead brother, and she adored him. On initially moving to Cornwall I'd had to face the fact that I was alone in the world, except for my son Jake, who was at that time living in Australia. On realising that I was a twin, and that I had a mother who was still alive, had been difficult for me to cope with. I was delighted of course and thrilled to find my new family, but from that solitary state to family relationships was not an easy transition to make. I read the text, *Mother gave me photo album. Possible link to our father!*

CHAPTER SIX

"Daisy, go and visit Violet. Remember to ask if she has heard anything about the murder. Your sister is local and may have heard information different from ours. I suggest we meet up an hour before the evening meal, and have a discussion about everything. Maybe by then we'll get more information from Tenby, possibly autopsy results," Jim said, as he too rose from his chair.

***

Martin agreed to take Flora back with him to the Priory. I took Lottie with me, she was now my constant companion. So it was about time that she met Sheba, my sister's German Shepherd dog, and Sheba should meet her. Only a short time ago, I had arrived one night in a storm at the Priory on Bodmin Moor. After a messy divorce, and the sale of my beloved family home, I was packing up my belongings when Cleo my rescue cat pushed a watercolour painting onto the floor. Hidden inside was a photograph of Wisteria cottage, and two women, with my name and birthdate on the back. Investigations threw up the facts that I was born in Cornwall, and Wisteria cottage where my sister now lived, was my original family home and where I had been born. Our mother had never, and would never divulge who our father had been. Born in a time when an illegitimate child was a shameful thing, Violet had been brought up as her mother's sister. I had been adopted by my aunt, who had then broken all ties with Cornwall and my family. Struggling with this new family setup came at a difficult time for me, trying to cope with my life as a divorced older woman.

***

I drew into the drive of Wisteria cottage and smiled to myself. Time to work out these family problems had been non-existent, the adventures in which we and the Priory had become involved with made sure of that! "Okay Lottie let's get you out of this harness. You are going to meet a big new friend. She's called Sheba, and I'm sure you're going to love each other." My words were optimistic, but I was not too sure.

Taking Lottie out of her harness I lifted her out, and cuddled her close to me. I don't know who I was trying to reassure, Lottie or myself. When I walked up the drive to the front door, I did have my fingers crossed, and was ready to grab Lottie and run. I needn't have bothered. I placed Lottie on the ground, keeping a tight grip on her lead. The front door opened, and my sister stood there with Sheba the large German Shepherd dog beside her. Lottie stood still and gazed at them both. But it was Sheba who reacted, she took one look at Lottie and fled!

"Thank goodness you could come at once! Come in here and look at this album." Violet was my quiet, staid sister. Not now, not at this moment. Excited, she grabbed my arm and pulled me in to the kitchen where an ancient photograph album lay upon the table. I sat down. She looked down at Lottie and smiled. Lottie had settled at my feet, stretched out, her head on her paws. She was exhausted after her lunchtime visit to the pub, and was already asleep.

"Sheba gets nervous when other dogs come into the house. She'll take a while to get used to Lottie, but once she does, I'm sure she'll love her to bits. I visited Mum this morning and she gave this to me. It's for both of us."

The kitchen faced out onto the gorgeous garden. Loved by generations of my family, it had developed into

24

a green oasis on this part of Bodmin Moor. A large conifer hedge screened most of the garden from the prevailing winds. This had enabled exotic plants which love the Cornish climate to flourish. They fringed the lawn which had a wonderful wildlife pond at one corner, and a covered patio, framed with wisteria over a loggia. I could see that the family had all been keen gardeners and my sister had followed in their footsteps, as the garden was immaculate. In the kitchen the yellow check curtains, and yellow chair pads were a bright and cheerful contrast to the grey day outside. The Aga gave off a welcome heat, and the red quarry tiled floor bore the imprints and scratches of generations of feet and scratchy paws. It was still so new to me, so difficult to understand and believe that here I had found my true family home.

Irritated by my lack of interest in the photo album and my contemplation of the garden, Violet thrust the open book in front of me. "Look, there's mother, and her sister, the one that brought you up, and three men. On the back there are names and the place where the photograph was taken. Do you think there's enough information there to find out who these men were and if any of them…?" Her voice drifted away. "I'm so sorry Daisy, I should never have texted you. It's such a feeble clue, I don't see how we can follow it up." Her face was a picture of misery, and I could see how much this really meant to her. I suppose it should have meant a lot to me, but I was still coming to grips with my mother and sister in my life. If I was honest with myself, I didn't really think that I could cope with a father! I hid my own feelings and pretended an enthusiasm that I really didn't feel.

I took the photograph out of the album. It had been placed in the old-fashioned corners that were stuck on the page, and the photograph was slotted inside. I put it on the table after staring at it, and the information written on the back. "If we go through the album, we can take notes of the men, the written information and put it all together. I'll take photos of each one of the ones we are interested in, and take them on my phone back with me to the Priory. Do you mind if I get the others in the Priory involved in the search? Martin and Sheila are brilliant on the Internet, I'll get them to look into it. They may well find something out for us. You are really keen on finding our father, aren't you Violet? Have you always wanted to find him?"

Violet looked at me for a moment. I could see she was thinking carefully about my questions. Violet would always think carefully I realized. Not like me, who had an impulsive streak. Pushing back a lock of her hair from her face, Violet took a deep breath. "Yes, I want to know, and time is not on our side. If anybody at the Priory can help us, that would be great."

We had both been so involved in the photo album and this deep conversation, we'd forgotten about the dogs. I turned round and looked at Sheba's basket. She was squashed in a corner of it. Lottie took up most of it, flat on her back, paws in the air and was snoring gently!

CHAPTER SEVEN

Lottie and I returned to my Priory cottage. Flora appeared with Martin when my van drew into the courtyard. "Flora was looking for you, I think she was missing you both." Flora and Lottie danced around us in a joyful reunion. "Everything okay Daisy?" Martin asked, knowing that I had rushed off to an urgent text from Violet.

"Yes Martin. Violet wanted… Can you come in a minute please? I need your expertise. It's raining now and these two are getting wet, and so are we." There was a sudden sharp shower and we all got drenched as we raced to my cottage. I gave Martin the doggy towel and he attempted to dry both dogs, which ended up in a three-way tug-of-war. "Leave them Martin. You've got the worst of the wet off them. We'll just have to put up with their doggy drying smell. Here's a mug of coffee for you, and a mug of tea for me. I'm desperate for mine, I can't cope with Violet's brew. It's so strong, I always refuse a cup, or pour it down the sink when her back is turned."

We both sipped at the hot beverages, then Martin put his down on the table. "What can I help you with Daisy?" Martin's shyness and his stammering had vanished as he got to know us. He was a loner with a fear of people. I wondered about his early childhood, and what trauma had led him to become such a recluse. He often spoke about his father with genuine affection, but his mother was only mentioned occasionally in passing.

I showed him the photos on my phone. "They're not like my photo that Cleo found. It had the photographer's name, and Wisteria cottage written on the back along with my mother and grandmother's names. There are few names here, and only the odd place name such as Polzeath beach."

A knock came at my door, and Jim entered. "Jim, can you help us? You managed to solve the Wisteria cottage photo with me." I repeated for Jim's benefit the little knowledge I had learnt from Violet. I thought back to Violet's urgent need to discover who our father was. Why was I not as keen as Violet? Knowing who my mother was, that she had loved me and have never wanted to give me away had been enough for me. A father who had abandoned a woman pregnant with his child was not someone I wished to meet.

But as I looked at Jim, I knew his mind was not wholly on our discussion. Somehow, and I did not like it, but I had become close to Jim. There had never been any discussion or understanding reached between us. Neither of us seemed to want to put into words what we were both feeling. Jim's reticence I assumed was because of his secretive past life. I was wary of committing my feelings to Jim because of my unfortunate marriage with Nigel. Jim had secrets he didn't want to share with me. I had a heart around which I had built a stone wall. But I knew that those feelings I had for Jim, enabled me to realize that Jim was either worried or had sustained a shock. Whatever this shock was, that was the reason Jim had come to my cottage. Something he wished to discuss with me. And only me!

I tuned back into the conversation between Martin and Jim. The photos looked at, the phone was handed back to me. "Martin, if you take the village where Violet's mum grew up, of course Daisy's mum as well, check any details you can for that name, in parish records, and census returns. Or whatever other list you can find. Check all the names from the photos, there may be a link," said Jim.

"Yes, there is the remote chance that they are all local people. Some generations have lived in the same houses in these villages for years." Martin agreed with Jim, his enthusiasm mounting. "Yes, that's one way forward. I'll go down that route immediately." He patted his beard and stroked the straggly wisp, jumped up from his chair, and raced back to his cottage and his computers.

When the door had closed behind Martin, I sat back in my chair and looked at Jim. "Okay Jim. Out with it. What's the matter?"

Jim rose to his feet, and he began to pace the floor. The animals who had been snuggled beside him on the sofa, sat up and watched him. My cottage was not built in the right shape for pacing up and down. The front lounge window to the back kitchen was not an adequate length for Jim's pacing. He managed it. I watched him and said nothing. The pets watched him for a while, but became bored when all Jim did was pace up and down and sigh. They fell asleep. What a good idea I thought, and envied them. Jim was worried. Not just worried, he was extremely worried. The Jim I had come to know in these few months had always seemed unflappable. We had been shot at and faced death, and usually the most he would do was raise that one eyebrow in concern. How that eyebrow infuriated me when it appeared. It often appeared when I'd done something stupid. I sat and watched the pacing. No way was I going to initiate this conversation! Whatever it was, and it was serious, it had to come from him.

The pacing stopped. Jim had reached a decision. His quick determined walk to the chair opposite me, and the way he sat down and faced me indicated that. "Thanks Daisy," he said.

I blinked. What did that mean?

He laughed at my bewilderment. "Thank you, Daisy, for not pestering me with questions. You always know when to keep quiet. A rare gift in anyone."

I sat quietly. But I was itching to get to my feet and yell at him to tell me what the hell the problem was!

"We all lunched at the Red Lion pub. You went to your sister Violet's house. I think the others came back to the Priory. I went to Stonebridge to do a quick shop. I've just returned. I entered my cottage and dumped my shopping down on the kitchen counter. That's when I knew. My cottage has been searched!"

CHAPTER EIGHT

"Searched? While you were out?" I stumbled over the words. My questions did little to frame the enormity of what Jim was saying. "Is there a mess? Or something stolen?"

"Daisy, nothing was stolen, and the place looks untouched. But for a few tricks of mine, which no one would expect or notice, I know that my cottage has been thoroughly and professionally searched!"

All I could do was stare at Jim. "Who would search your place? And why?" Jim got up and looked as if he was going to start the pacing thing all over again. He sat back down. He ran a hand through his white hair, an action that I'd never seen him do before. A sign of extreme stress and worry I thought.

"It's a professional search, no doubt someone from my old days. What they are looking for I don't know. I've been out of the business for some time. When I left there were no loose ends. No vendettas to come back and haunt me. There is no reason that I can think of, as to why someone was searching my cottage." Jim sat staring into space.

"Have you checked your cottage with your bug thingy," I asked him.

His deep worry lines vanished, and he smiled at me. "Daisy how do you do it? You always go straight to the most practical point. Yes, I've used the bug thingy, but it is a basic one. This was a pro job, if bugs have been planted in my cottage, I need a more up-to-date bug thingy." Jim shuffled his feet and took a deep breath before he spoke. "I want to ask you something Daisy. I don't think there's any danger, but you can refuse me if you are worried. Are you willing to help me Daisy?"

"Of course, I'll help you, Jim. What do you want me to do?" Visions of myself toting guns, using secret spy equipment, and perhaps having an ankle holster flashed through my mind. These visions were squashed by his next words and faded away, admittedly with some regret.

"I'd like to use your phone to order equipment. Mine might be compromised. Can I have parcels delivered to your cottage? I'll order some burner phones, and perhaps other equipment." Jim was talking out loud, concocting a plan for action. Jim would not sit quietly and wait for the next occurrence. No, Jim had to act. I got up and went to the kitchen and came back with my shopping pad and pen, and gave it to him to compile a list. Returning to the kitchen I put the kettle on, I needed yet another mug of tea. Jim needed something stronger I thought, and poured him out a whisky. On my return to the lounge, I found a happier looking Jim with a long list written out in front of him.

"I'd like to use your phone now Daisy." A look of embarrassment crossed his face, and he continued speaking, "do you mind if I take it privately?"

"Take it in my bedroom, you'll get peace from the dogs as well, they may well bark and disrupt your call."

Sometime later, Jim walked back out with my phone in his hand, and smiled at me. "I contacted a couple of my old friends. One is still active in the service, the other has a desk job now. Both will investigate from their end, to see if they can work out who is actually looking into me and my activities. Equipment is being organized by them and will be posted immediately. I'm delighted as it will be top grade military quality. I won't be caught out again. If there's a return visit, I will be ready." Jim relaxed back into the sofa and began to drink his whisky.

"Are you okay now Jim?" I asked him.

Jim swallowed the last of the whisky in one huge gulp.

"Yes, I'm fine now. Speaking to my friends, and knowing they are going to look into the matter has helped tremendously."

We finished our drinks, and realised it was time to go to the Priory for the Investigation discussion.

***

"What about the others? Do you want to tell them or not?" I asked as we walked across the courtyard to the Priory kitchen.

"No Daisy, just you for the moment. I don't want to worry the others, and there's not much to tell them. If I think it'll affect any of them or you, I'll tell them. Daisy, I can't thank you enough for being here for me. Thank you, Daisy." Jim stopped, turned me to face him and put his hand on my shoulder. "Thanks." That was all Jim said, but there was a depth of meaning in that gesture and in his eyes. A long moment passed between us as we looked at each other.

CHAPTER NINE

Why couldn't I sleep? My night was punctuated by weird dreams. They had no discernible shape or form, rather my sleep was punctuated by imaginings of a frightening nature. Exhausted, I roused myself from the last patchy doze which had claimed me after dawn. It was breakfast time, not that I was hungry, but the 'guys' were waiting anxiously. Always fed, or overfed according to their vet, they were fretful if their meal was not forthcoming at the usual time. All three of them had lives before I took them on, meals may not have been regular in their past. The kettle was on, the animals fed, and I opened the back door for them to go out in the garden. Another crisp morning, with the slight sprinkle of frost disappearing fast in the sunlight. The early morning light across the moorland and the trees close to the kitchen garden was wonderful. I breathed deeply, enjoying the clarity and purity of the Cornish air. Spikes of green were thrusting their way up through the frosty earth. The borders were only narrow strips around the lawn, and a few paving slabs outside the kitchen door was my patio. Dreams of a summer garden filled with flowers, tubs of cascading climbers and a patio complete with an elegant table and chairs vanished at the sound of an incoming text. *Parcels coming shortly to your cottage. Okay? J.* I replied immediately, *Okay I'm up.* Jim's friends had obviously leapt into action and his spy type goodies were arriving shortly.

***

I made a mug of tea, got the animals in, and raced to my bedroom to dress. Comfortable, and practical warm clothes would be best, as it promised to be a busy day. I threw on top of my jeans a new purple and lime green jacket with panels of embroidery down the front. Was it too dressy? Too glitzy for everyday wear? I stood in front of the mirror debating, my shy blend into the background persona, was raising her head again... No! I'm wearing it. I want to wear it whether it's too dressy or not.

Decision made I wandered back into the kitchen and made toast and scrambled eggs. The plate went into the dishwasher. I put on my coat and got the two leads and harness for the dogs. Walks with the dogs were not as frantic as they had been, both dogs walked well for me now, and we only got tangled up every few minutes, not all the time.

***

My phone rang in my coat pocket, and when I took it out and saw it was Jake, my mood immediately lifted. Jake my son, always brightened my day. He was staying with his fiancée and her parents at Bude. They were looking forward to settling down into his newly inherited cottage on Bodmin Moor. When I had discovered my birth mother some weeks ago, Jake as the male heir had inherited a cottage. About to be married to Lisa, it had been a wonderful surprise. Habitable, but in dire need of updating after the long tenure of an elderly lady, they were about to embark upon it when Lisa's father became ill again. A few weeks ago, a drunk driver had left him with injuries of a broken arm and severely gashed leg. Last week he had become ill again, and it seemed that he had sustained internal injuries which had been previously overlooked.

"Mum, is everything okay with you?" My assurance that nothing had happened, and everything was just as usual was said with my fingers crossed. It was just as usual, we were always having murders, burglaries and general mayhem here, so it wasn't really a lie. "Lisa's father is pretty bad again. I'm going to have to stay here for a while. Lisa is finding it hard to cope with the uncertainty over her dad, and her mother's completely collapsed over it all." Encouraging words and good wishes from me and the reassurance that all was fine here, and we finished our call. Jake and Lisa had been in Australia, gold digging, and their return after Liza's brush with a snake, was brought forward at the news of her father's accident. Jake seemed to be living round the corner now to me after that long distance away in Australia. A swift recovery for Lisa's father, and they could get to work on the cottage.

My walk had been around the kitchen garden and partly down the lane. I hadn't forgotten the imminent arrival of Jim's parcels and needed to be on hand to receive them. This walk meant I could see the delivery van and return home quickly. I wondered if Jim would let me look in the parcels. Would he let me play with some of his high-tech gadgets? I hoped so, but realistically knew that he wouldn't. The parcels hadn't come when I returned to my cottage. I gave the dogs their treats, and a special pussy cat treat for Cleo, and settled them in their baskets. "Time for me to go for tea in the Priory kitchen. I can hear and see any delivery van that comes into the courtyard from the kitchen," I told them.

***

The usual warmth from the Aga was blissful after the cold morning outside. Demelza was in today, our deputy housekeeper, as she liked to be called. A local lady, in her late forties, she came in to help Maggie three days a week. Still beautiful, she always wore black, and always with a touch of lace somewhere. The black lace gave her an exotic look, which together with the zigzag scar down her cheek made her a striking beauty despite her age. On first meeting me, she had claimed I was a family member. To everyone's surprise, Demelza had proved right, we were cousins. Her only idiosyncrasy, and we never, ever understood why, but she always wore white wellington boots. She smiled as usual, but there were shadows under her eyes, and her usual bouncy cheerfulness was non-existent.

I took my place at the kitchen table, my usual place. How quickly we had fallen into that habit of having our places. Jim always sat with his back to the wall, facing all entrances and exits anywhere and everywhere he went. Spy training, I guessed. I liked facing the window and seeing the far distant hills. Sheila loved being in the middle of all of us. Today she sat there with her Agenda book open at today's date.

"What are we going to do today? We must plan something, or it will be boring. A murder and we have no information about it. We don't have any clues! How are we going to get any today? It's vital we get some now, the hours after a murder are crucial to get clues. Otherwise, they disappear or something," Sheila said.

"There was no news from the hairdressers, you tried that Sheila. I suppose we could try the pub that Roy went to, but he wasn't a regular, so I don't think we'll get much there. It's not like the puppy farm, there were so many avenues to explore," Jim replied.

Demelza was subdued again and moved about the kitchen as if in a daze. Although flamboyant and outgoing normally, there was a private almost secretive side to Demelza. The questions I longed to ask her, I felt sure would not be welcomed. Demelza would tell me if there was a problem, wouldn't she? After all, as she often told me we were family. I watched her out of the corner of my eye a while longer. No, if it continued, I would ask her. With that settled in my mind, I watched Sheila open her agenda book and draw a line under the days date.

"Nothing from my hairdressers visit. Nothing much at the pub. Where else could we find about Roy's doings? I know Daisy and Jim are going to see Arthur, what can the rest of us investigate? And where?"

"Is it worth asking questions from people on his postal round? How could we do that without getting Tenby mad at us?" I asked.

Demelza turned round towards us. "I know Roy stopped off at a few folks for a cuppa and a chat. He was a real gossip and loved to know what was going on in the village. The two people he was most often seen visiting were Mrs. Evans and Joan Perkins. Real gossips they are, and Joan Perkins can be vicious with it! But they would know what he was up to, if anyone would."

"What would we say? We can't just arrive on their doorsteps," I said.

"Daisy is correct, we must have an excuse to visit them," agreed Jim.

"The village hall fund!" Maggie said. "Next Saturday there is going to be a fair in the hall. All proceeds to go for roof repairs and new toilets. There will be a grand raffle, and I have been given loads of raffle ticket books to sell. They will give you the perfect excuse. Please take some of these!" Maggie walked over to her bag on the counter and pulled out a pile of raffle ticket books. These she plonked down in front of Jim with a look of satisfaction.

"Perfect, we have an excuse now to call upon anyone we want," said Jim.

Demelza's phone rang. She took it out of her pocket.

Everyone in the kitchen could hear the frantic cries and almost hysterical voice coming over her phone. "Wait a minute, Mary. Calm down and speak slowly." The voice at the other end gave a distinct sob, and there was silence. Demelza walked over to the table, and placed the phone down in front of us after pressing the speaker button. "Oh Demelza, they found the poison. I've got to go to the police station for questioning. Demelza what am I going to do? I didn't kill him. But they found the poison in the garden shed. I've never seen it before. It was an old bottle of stuff to kill moles! Demelza what am I going to do? They are going to arrest me for murdering Roy."

CHAPTER TEN

"Don't worry Mary. We'll investigate further, we'll sort it out." The frantic voice came through the phone, "I've got to go now Demelza. Please, you've got to help me!" The phone went dead. Demelza picked it up and put it in her pocket. "What happens now?" Hands on her hips, she glared at us. "You lot had better get a move on. Mary is going to have a breakdown, and worst of all she's going to be charged with murder."

"Demelza, tell Mary we're working on it, we'll follow up with the raffle tickets this morning, and visit Arthur this afternoon," said Jim.

"What will I do? Martin wants to help as well, we all do. Not one of us wants to see poor Mary banged up in jail," said Sheila.

"At the moment, there seems little that you can do Sheila. What about helping Daisy out with that family history search. I know Daisy isn't that worried about it, but her sister Violet is very keen to get started on the search for their father. Whilst Daisy and I attend to this legwork, would you mind doing some Internet searches for Daisy?"

"I'd be so grateful Sheila, I wouldn't worry about it so much, but Violet is convinced that we will find our father too late. She is convinced that he will be dead before we find him, and so she thinks it's absolutely urgent to get going on this search. Honestly Sheila, I wouldn't know where to start on the Internet for this stuff. I've tried going on Ancestry, but I get muddled up with all the dates and names."

Sheila smiled at me. "Okay Daisy, I've seen your research notes. They leave a lot to be desired! I'll do that if it saves you all the bother. But it's only until we find something that I can do connected with this murder. Is that understood? Is that understood by everyone?" Sheila directed a suspicious glare at Jim.

He lifted his hands in surrender. "Okay Sheila, it's only a temporary task. Will that satisfy you?"

"Okay, now have you got maps sorted out? Do you know the roads that you have to go down to reach Joan Perkins and Mrs. Evans?"

When Jim and I looked at Sheila and shook our heads, there was a heavy sigh from her, and she went to the computer. "I've got the roads now that they live on from Demelza, I'll just print off a map of the village and mark on their places of residence."

At the phrase places of residence, Jim's eyes met mine, and we both turned away from each other trying to stifle giggles. Sheila was wonderful, but often her expressions were strange, and we had to smile, but we couldn't let her see us smile. We loved her too much. The map was printed out, two large crosses marked the important visits we had to make, and this was presented with a flourish to us by Sheila. On the top of the map in large block capital letters were the words Operation Raffle Ticket.

"Martin and I will make a start on your family history Daisy. But the moment you find that you need our help on the investigation, we'll stop immediately," Sheila said.

"Sheila, when we need your help, you will certainly drop that at once." I reassured our octogenarian who I realised felt that her increasing age and lack of mobility was keeping her from the more fun aspects of our investigations. I made a firm promise to myself that in future I would find interesting parts of our investigation, and make certain that Sheila was right in the middle of them.

As we walked out of the courtyard to my van, Jim

laughed and repeated Sheila's words. "Here we go on Operation Raffle Ticket!" It had been decided, by Jim of course, that we should drive round the streets selling the raffle tickets in my van. It's conspicuous logo of BURT'S BEEFY BANGERS was a good focal point, and if any information was forthcoming from anyone in the future they'd know where to bring it. I wasn't too sure that I wanted odd bods turning up at my cottage with dubious information. But I knew it wasn't worth arguing the point. Jim thought it a great idea, and maybe it was. As I got ready to drive out of the courtyard and underneath the archway I also repeated Sheila's words. "Let Operation Raffle Ticket begin!"

Whatever was going to be said by Jim in reply was interrupted by the delivery van entering the courtyard. It took only seconds and Jim dashed over to the van. I got out more slowly, and smiled at Jim's enthusiastic welcome to the delivery man. The boxes were not large. Several were marked fragile, and these Jim grabbed from the delivery man and carried them in carefully himself. He deposited them on the kitchen counter. Shoebox size, the majority of them sat side-by-side. The two marked fragile were smaller than the others. These Jim pounced on, and when I passed him my kitchen scissors, he cut the tape and carefully opened the first one. The gadget he lifted out of the box, he held it reverently in his hand, and pressed a button. A light came on. Holding it in his hand, and with his hand outstretched he walked round my cottage downstairs. Then he gestured to the upstairs. When I nodded, he proceeded to climb the stairs still holding the gadget and sweeping it from side to side. Jim returned downstairs. "All clear, I thought it would be. I'm going to check my cottage and my car before I do anything else. Okay if I leave this lot here for a moment?"

"Fine by me," I said and looked at Jim's parcels after he'd gone. They were so tempting. I remembered shaking parcels when I was small, under the Christmas tree. These were not to be shaken. I'd either damage some delicate mechanism or they might explode in my face. I took my kitchen notepad and sat at the table and began making notes. Perhaps I needed a special notebook, something between Sheila's Agenda book with its cover of pet photos, and the Executive notebook that Jim used. I smiled at my own foolishness and made a list. The cottages with our prospective interviewees were listed. I had thought to make notes of what information we'd obtain from them. I'd nearly finished the list when Jim walked in the door.

Jim's face was a mixture of fury and dismay, and could I detect a tinge of fear? "Three bugs, one in my car, one in the lounge and one in the kitchen area. They were sophisticated and minute, and extremely well hidden, no wonder my other detector missed them." Jim began pacing up and down. Again! "These bugs that were planted are the most sophisticated bugs obtainable, they are not even on the black market. Either it's a sanctioned operation by some agency, such as MI6 or even the CIA, or they were planted by someone with the contacts to be able to get this stuff. Why are they targeting me? Why now? I'm out of the business. I've been out of it for years." Again, the restless hand went through his hair. Jim flung himself into an armchair and stared at me. "Daisy, I'm at a complete loss. I don't know what to do!"

Nor did I. Never had I seen Jim such a state. Even when he had been shot and was bleeding in agony, and was facing possible death down the gun barrel. Even then he had not looked so worried or frightened.

"What have you done about the bugs," I asked him.

"I left them in place, then they don't know I've

discovered them and know I'm being watched. We'll just have to be careful what is said in there, but as I'm doing and saying nothing secretive, that's no problem."

"Your friends are still investigating on your behalf?" I asked him. At his murmured reply I continued. "Nothing else you can do, except unwrap each of these parcels and sort them all out. Then we have to go and sell some raffle tickets!" I stood up, reached a hand towards him to pull him up to his feet.

Jim was up in seconds, my hand held tightly, and his arm came around me. He hugged me and kissed me lightly on my cheek. "Thanks Daisy. I don't know what I'd do without you." He murmured gruffly in my ear and walked quickly to unwrap the parcels. I watched him, his back retreating, with my mouth open. What had just occurred?

***

Sometime later we had put the paper and cardboard safely into the recycling bin. There was an array of instruments on my kitchen counter. Some were small, others large but they all looked technical, important, and somehow carried an aura of malice. "Can I keep them here Daisy? I don't want to take them back to my cottage. My visitors may return."

I opened the kitchen cupboard. "How about if I emptied this for you? Or do you need something more secure?"

"No, this is ideal. If we place them behind the packets and tins, that will defeat a cursory search."

It was done speedily between us. The thought that someone might do a search through my cottage, even if it was going to be a cursory one was not only unsettling but frightening.

"There are recording devices, cameras and GPS trackers in that lot. It's easy enough for me to reach them if I have to act fast," Jim said, after his stuff was stowed away.

"Right Jim, it's off to…"

"Sell raffle tickets. Okay Daisy, let's go."

Jim's colour was better, that 'turn' for want of a better word had gone. Enthusing over his equipment that had been sent to him by his friend, had restored his equilibrium. The old Jim was back. We gave the animals some treats and promised them a walk on our return. As we walked out of the courtyard to my van, Jim laughed and repeated Sheila's words. "Here we go on Operation Raffle Ticket!"

CHAPTER ELEVEN

"The routes are planned out. We should take it methodically, but making certain that Mrs. Evans and Joan Perkins are done this morning. Their information we'll get as soon as possible, so that we can help Mary's defense," I said. Remembering the map Sheila had printed for us, I drove my van down the main street of the village before turning into a small cul-de-sac. "I see Mrs. Evans lives in the third house along. Let's start first at the neighbours." A chatty older man bought two raffle tickets. He knew all about the leaking roof, and was quite pleased to buy a raffle ticket. He had quite a little chat with us, and when I left I wondered who else he would talk to that day. Or that week. Our visit had been a pleasant surprise to him, and it only cost him a couple of raffle tickets. At the next house there was no reply. "Now for Mrs. Evans," I muttered, and walked down the path. Neat borders surrounded a crazy paved area. The gravel path gave warning of our arrival, and the door was flung open before Jim even knocked.

"What do you want? Why are you knocking on people's doors?" The figure was stout and encased in an old-fashioned apron, her hair tightly permed, and dyed an improbable black. Immediately I was transported to those 1950's adverts which pictured the ideal housewife. No happy smiling face here though. A thin mouth was drawn back over yellowed teeth, and she gave us a watery smile. I noted the net curtain at the nearby window still had a crease in it from where she had obviously watched our arrival at her neighbour's door.

Jim launched into his village hall speech but was interrupted before he'd even got going. "You're those people from the Priory, aren't you? I know that sausage van belongs to you. What are you doing up here? Why are you bothering us folks here?"

Nonplussed by this attack, and uncertain as to which question he should answer first, Jim paused before speaking.

I stepped in. "We're sorry to bother you, but we're selling raffle tickets in aid of the village hall repairs. Your neighbour bought two from us," I added, hoping to spur her into buying some.

"Ha, did he, only two. Come on in then and I will buy three. Need to find my purse." As we walked into the hall and stood there, I noticed a torn envelope and letter flung onto the hall table. The writing was in green ink. I nudged Jim and inclined my head towards it. He was standing right beside it. Moving in front of him I followed her a little way down the hall, blocking Jim from her view.

"This is so generous of you Mrs...."

"Evans, I'm Hilda Evans, that's me," came the reply, and she appeared again with her purse and pen. Writing her name on the raffle ticket slip, she then gave us the money, and we turned to leave. Neither Jim nor I had managed to find a way to chat further with Hilda, or to introduce the murder. Mrs. Evans however, realizing her captive audience was about to leave, suddenly launched into speech herself. "Dreadful business up there at the Priory. Were you there when Roy's body was found?"

"Oh yes," I said and shuddered. "Yes, it's sad that he was murdered, he was still quite a young man," I added to the conversation.

"Oh no! Not a shame that he was murdered. It's a shame that the body was discovered. His killer deserved a medal not a prison sentence. He rid the world of an evil man, that's what he did. We're all better off without that Roy Jones!" At our astonishment, she gave a little laugh and lifted the letter and waved it in our faces. "That man was evil. Pure evil. He found out secrets, steaming open the envelopes, and then he blackmailed people in return for his silence. Tried it on with me. I got this letter this morning. I heard that he died earlier this morning, so he can't hurt me now. But if he had lived, I would have found some way to make him pay, that I would. Thought he knew everyone's secrets did Roy. But I knew one of his. One that he would have paid me to keep quiet! Yes, thought he was clever, ferreting out people's secrets. But I knew his big secret, and he wouldn't have liked that to be common gossip in the village!" Her voice rose in excited justification and anger. Holding the letter, she was now waving it wildly in our faces.

"If you know something about him, some secret he had, you should tell the police. It may help them," said Jim.

"No!" It was a forceful and loud reply, which took us both aback. "No. Whoever killed him did me and quite a few others a favour. I'm not giving help in getting him put away. Should give whoever it was killed that Roy a medal." At that last remark, she almost pushed us out of the door, slamming it in our faces.

**

We walked down the path in a stunned silence. I turned towards Jim. "What do you make of that? What do you think the secret was? If only she had told us. I couldn't see a way to get it out of her, could you?" So, Hilda Evans had a secret, and she knew one of Roy Jones's secrets. And that secret had been serious enough she had said, to blackmail him. We went to the next few doors selling raffle tickets, because we couldn't make it too obvious that Hilda Evans had been our target. We were desperate to find out what was in the letter that Jim had photographed. Nevertheless we went through the motions explaining what the raffle tickets were for, taking the money and thanking each person politely and warmly for their generosity. I wasn't certain what Jim was thinking about, but I knew that my mind was fizzing.

"What the hell could that secret be?" Jim said as we got in the van and drove away. I parked in a layby beside the open moorland. "What can Roy Jones have done that he wanted hidden from everybody. How did Hilda Evans find it out?"

"Never mind that, what did you see in the letter?" I turned to Jim eagerly. "What was in that letter that Hilda Evans waved in our face?"

Jim shook his head, and fiddled with his phone. "That was quick thinking of yours Daisy. I realised what you meant when you nodded to the letter lying open on the hall table. I've got it here; it came up as a clear photo."

CHAPTER TWELVE

There was an intake of breath from him as he realized what the letter said. "She was pilfering money from church funds! She had been taking some of the flower money each week, and skimming money out of the roof fund when she was supposed to be counting it."

"But it can't have been that much money, surely?" I asked Jim, surprised at the tone of his voice.

He shook his head at me. "It's not the money that's important. It would be the lack of trust in her by the members of the church, and everyone in the village. Her life would be ruined if anyone knew about this. No wonder she was furious with Roy. I can understand why she was delighted someone killed him."

"If only we could've found out what the secret was that she knew about Roy. It would've given us possibly a motive for someone else other than Mary." We drove on in a thoughtful silence.

Jim looked at his watch, "Not bad going for only twenty minutes, I think we've got time before lunch to try for Joan Perkins." Remembering the plan and the cottages where Joan Perkins lived, I drove on.

***

A few minutes later we parked outside the row of three cottages. The gardens sloped down from a bank to the road, and the three cottages were set high above the road nestling into the hillside. "Joan lives in the middle one, it's the one with the blue door. Let's go and see what she has to say. She may know nothing to help us in the investigation. But if we can get some money for the church fund that will be something, even if we get no information." I said as we stood beside the car, looking at them. The cottages were terraced, but each one was very different. They each had their own distinct appearance, reflecting the owners personality. Facing us, the one on the right had a badly mown lawn, weedy flowerbeds, and an array of kayaks, canoes, and surfboards all arranged under a carport, on the drive and spreading onto the lawn. The left-hand one had a beautifully mown lawn with regimented stripes on it. The flowers were arranged in neat rows, all colour coordinated. This was a property that had been beautifully presented and maintained.

"Wow!" The word escaped me as I stared dumbfounded at the middle-terraced cottage. A sloping path wound its way up to the front door. Not a neat series of steps like its neighbours. Oh no, this wound crazily around the front garden. Fronting the pavement a row of ducks stood like sentries. They were multicolored. It was the pink one with the blue bill and the bright yellow eyes and feet that really stood out. It was larger than the rest and had an angry face, and looked as if it was challenging us. I'll swear its bill curled in contempt at us. Along both edges of the path were a multitude of woodland creatures, there were rabbits, squirrels and even a couple of deer. There was no lawn in this garden, it was shingle and crazy paving with pink glittery mosaic chips dotted amongst it. In little companion groups, gnomes sat, fished, and gardened complete with rakes, buckets and spades. Beside them toadstools of varying colors and heights added to the bizarre scene in front of us.

My sidelong glance at Jim nearly had me doubled up in laughter. Never since I had met him had I seen him so flabbergasted. Speechless, he stood his mouth open as if he was about to speak but the words would not come. There were no words available in any dictionary. It was a garden that literally took your breath away! Without comment we made for the first cottage. The neatly regimented house and garden had for its owner as one would expect a neatly regimented man. Clad in shirt and trousers, these casual garments took on a neatness and pristine appearance not usually found worn around the house. The crease in his trousers was knife sharp, and his shirt had such a neatly ironed appearance, that it looked as if it was wearing him, not the other way around. He kindly bought a couple of raffle tickets, and commented on the weather, and the necessity of the church hall repairs.

Taking a deep breath and giving each other a reassuring look, Jim led the way up the winding path between the gnomes and woodland creatures. Jim knocked at the door and we both stood back. There was music playing somewhere in the cottage, it sounded like hymns. We waited for someone to come. We hadn't really discussed how we would approach the subject of the dead body of Roy. It wasn't an easy thing to throw into a casual conversation. As it was a major talking point in the village, we could only hope that perhaps she would raise the subject. Suddenly the door was opened. She was a big woman, with broad shoulders and a plain face that twisted into dislike when she realized who stood on her doorstep.

"What do you want?" The words were flung at us. Her mouth twisted nastily for a moment, an unbelievable moment when I was convinced that she was going to spit at me. "Well, what do you want?"

"We're selling raffle tickets for the church roof fund." Jim's voice faded away as a snort of laughter greeted his remark.

"Both of you are selling raffle tickets for the church! You should both be in that church on your knees confessing your sins. Evil sinners, that's what you are. All those living at the Priory are stained with the Devil's deeds!"

Jim stood his ground in the face of these accusations, but I stepped back. This sudden outburst from the woman was unexpected, and quite frankly horrifying. But she followed me, a gnarled wavering finger pointing at me.

"You are that woman. You're the one that rides around in the van with that silly fat man on the side encouraging gluttony. You're the one that wears stupid bright clothes." Her eyes raked me up and down, every bright item of my clothing registering with her as something evil. "Flaunting yourself at your age. Evil! You are nothing but a tart. An elderly fallen woman, who will perish for her evil actions in hellfire." The voice rose ending in a shriek. Spittle flew from her mouth as her words tumbled out in rage. The black shapeless dress hung on the large woman. Her brown brogues with sensible rubber soles, were a silent reproach to my navy and brown leather boots with stylish embossed flowers and leather tassels. I could feel my confidence, my newfound confidence drifting away in the wind at this virulent outburst from a complete stranger.

That last remark was said with such venom and spite that I took an involuntary step backwards. Only one little step backwards, but what a catastrophe unfolded as a result! Struggling to keep my balance my arms flailed about. My hand unwittingly hit the large gnome planter beside me. Grabbing for something to break my fall I clutched at his pointed hat.

"Daisy! Take care, Daisy!" Jim shouted at me.

CHAPTER THIRTEEN

"Wolfgang! My darling Wolfgang! What have you done to him? Leave him alone!" Shrieked Joan Perkins.

The gnome Wolfgang and his pointed hat did not save me. Both he and I began to fall onto the shingle front garden. And hovered on the edge of the steep slope. Wolfgang crashed beside me, and shattered his face. The large bulbous nose flew off, rolling over and over down between the gnomes and toadstools to land at the feet of the pink duck. The duck's sneer grew more pronounced, and it gazed in distaste at the nose resting on its webbed feet. The leering grin ended up beside me, and minus his nose gave Wolfgang a weird satanic look. The bulbs in the compost flew out from his planter around us in a wide arc clattering onto the shingle.

Jim had moved quickly, and his hand gripping my arm prevented me from fully landing onto the ground and rolling downhill. My other hand flung out in time upon a large red spotted toadstool also supported me. He pulled me to my feet, anxiety warring on his face with laughter.

"You all right Daisy? That could have been a bad tumble."

"Thanks Jim. You saved me from landing completely on the ground. I'm all right, but I think I twisted my ankle. The weak one of course."

"You may be all right, but Wolfgang isn't! His nose! You've broken his nose! You've knocked it off, and it's rolled all the way down to the road. His lederhosen have all been scratched where he's landed on the stones. You are an evil woman! A destructive evil woman!"

A single yank on my arm by Jim, and he raced down the winding path. His continued pressure on my arm facilitated my speedy exit down the path and into the van.

Her shouts became screams, and I could see her follow us into the middle of the road, shaking her fist at our retreating van.

***

Despite my nervous shaking and shock after my near disaster, I managed to drive away. When I came back to the layby where I had stopped earlier, I drew in to catch my breath and recover.

"So that is Joan Perkins. That woman needs help. I think she is well worth investigating. I can see her killing Roy Jones without a qualm, can't you?" I said. My words were jerky as I kept trying to breathe after the confrontation.

Jim looked at me, really looked at me. "Oh no Daisy! You didn't let those words of that woman get to you? She's obviously a bitter twisted woman. Don't let the words she flung at you destroy that confidence that you are slowly building up."

I knew Jim realized that I was constantly in need of reassurance. Years of Nigel, my ex-husbands belittling remarks had destroyed the confident young girl I had been when I married him. After my divorce, and my move down to Cornwall, my confidence had been slowly reasserting itself. It was astute of Jim to understand that even now it didn't take much to pull me back down into my shy persona. I gave him a weak smile. We drove back to the Priory for lunch, all thoughts of knocking on any doors to sell more raffle tickets that morning had gone! A quick sandwich in my kitchen, and I gave the pets their lunch, and let them out in the garden. I arranged for Martin to walk Flora and Lottie later, whilst Jim and I went to visit the retired postman Arthur. Jim had grabbed a snack from his own cottage, whilst checking again for further bugs or unwanted visitors.

***

Thirty minutes later we were on our way to sell raffle tickets at the couple of semi-detached cottages beside the bridge. We knew Arthur, the retired postman was living in number six. Our plan was to call at number four, so making all our visits ostensibly raffle ticket ones. There was no one in at number four, so we went down the narrow path to number six where Arthur lived. Our strategy had been planned out in the van as we drove there. We had agreed that Jim should do the talking at first, that might be best for an older man.

***

The door was opened at our first knock. An old man lent heavily on a stick, he looked frail and fragile. His eyes brightened at Jim's mention of the raffle tickets, and it was with immense pleasure he invited us in. We refused his kind offer of a drink but accepted his invitation to sit down. He bustled about finding some money for the raffle tickets, commenting all the time on the need for the repairs. Both of us smiled and murmured suitable replies. Eventually his need for talk wound down, and he finally sat. This was what Jim had been waiting for. I saw Jim think carefully of how to phrase his inquiries. The old man was pleased to have company, but I think we both realized that he was no fool, and certainly was still very alert.

"I expect you have heard about Roy Jones?" Jim said.

"Yes, not surprised he came to a sticky end. Always caused trouble, even when he was a kid. But he was never caught out, although he always started the trouble.

Roy stepped back and let others take the blame. My old mother always said that he made the snowballs, but gave them to other people to throw." His final remark caused him to laugh uproariously. We joined in with the laughter.

"Did you know that Mary his wife is being blamed for his murder?" Jim said.

"No! That Mary wouldn't say boo to a goose. She could never kill him, not Mary." Arthur was horrified at the very idea.

"We wondered if you knew anything about him that would help in clearing Mary's name. Any little thing might be helpful," said Jim.

"Got really bad arthritis I have," said Arthur.

"Arthritis, that can be very painful," I replied. I began to wonder if the old man wasn't as alert as I had imagined him to be. What did arthritis have to do with proving Mary's innocence?

"Yes, that Roy used to help me out in the garden. Because of my arthritis I couldn't mow the lawn or weed the beds. Always kept a nice, neat garden, upset me it did when I couldn't cope anymore. I couldn't afford to pay a gardener as I told Roy, but he came up with a plan."

"A plan?" Jim and I both bent forward, eager to hear what this plan was.

"Down the bottom of my garden, I have a shed. It's divided into two parts, one part is for all my gardening tools, and the lawnmower. The other part was for my hobbies. Don't use it anymore, too tiring going down that hill in all weathers. Played havoc with the aches and pains."

I didn't dare look at Jim, I knew his face would mirror my own in its blank incomprehension. Was there a point to this rambling conversation? If there was, I wish Arthur would get to it.

"Roy did all my gardening, and I let him use the shed. He even bought a large padlock for it. Said did I mind if he kept it locked. Didn't matter to me, he could put as many padlocks on it as he liked."

"I wonder if there is anything in there that would help clear Mary's name. Could we go and look please?" I asked the old man. One look at Jim's face and I felt I had to speak. Jim was stunned, and almost unable to speak at this astonishing discovery.

"But it's locked. If you can get into it, you're welcome. Do anything I would to help that poor lass out. Don't want her locked up in prison over that scoundrel."

The old man had hardly finished his sentence before we were out of the door, and racing down the garden to the shed.

CHAPTER FOURTEEN

Jim's long legs meant that he reached the shed before me. When I came up to him, he had already taken out his little wallet of lock picking tools. Jim stood looking at the padlock for some time, then got out his phone and photographed it. "Someone has been here before us. It's been tampered with, there are scratch marks on it." He made quick work of opening the padlock. As I stood watching him, I realized that the old man had approached us and was standing behind me. The journey from his kitchen down to the shed had obviously tired him out.

Arthur smiled at me. "I've always wanted to see what he was doing in that shed. I always thought he just needed a place to relax, and that he was probably drinking a beer, you know, something like that." His voice betrayed the worry that had now taken hold of him. He had known Roy Jones for years, a work colleague, a neighbour, someone who he thought he could trust. Why wouldn't he let him use his shed? Why wouldn't he be grateful for the exchange? The backbreaking work of his garden had been taken care off, in exchange for the use of this shed.

"Done it. But that padlock was state-of-the-art. An expensive one for just a garden shed. Let's see what was so important that it needed to be so well kept hidden," said Jim.

What I found so amazing as we filed into that shed one after the other, was how neat and tidy it was. Somehow, I had a vision of a dusty dirty shed, with cobwebs in the far corners and grimy windows. No, it was almost pristine in its cleanliness and neatness. The inside windows were not grimy, they sparkled. A long table was placed beneath one of the windows. At one side was placed a kettle, and industrial size tweezers, several plates and a large box of tissues. Midway down the table were open letters and their envelopes, obviously placed to dry out. The far end of the table was piled high with unopened letters. On one wall there were photocopies of letters with accompanying notes of names and addresses. A large book was on a shelf beneath these. All three of us said nothing, we just stood open mouthed looking about the place. I noticed Jim reaching for his phone. Dozens of clicks followed, as he walked round taking photos of everything. He glanced at me and motioned to the old man. I understood and gently guided Arthur out of the door.

"We'd better call the police, they will want to see this," I said and guided him back into his kitchen. As he sat down heavily on his chair, I phoned Tenby. Suddenly, the old man had aged in that moment when he realized what his shed been used for. I waited for the kettle to boil, and through the kitchen window watched Jim through the open shed door. He had put gloves on, and then rifled through the book on the shelf, and looked through further boxes, his phone clicking away.

Tenby arrived, and it was sometime later that we were allowed to go. He saw through our raffle tickets excuse, but said nothing. How could he? If it hadn't been for us, the inside of that shed might not have been discovered for some considerable time. Even if the old man had found it all, he may not have realized the full importance of the stuff inside. No, much as he disliked us finding the interior of the shed and its vital evidence, Tenby could only be delighted at having it all in his hands.

***

"It still doesn't let Mary off the hook, you know. Roy was downright evil, some of those letters held important secrets. He must've put those poor people through hell. Especially in a village where gossip can be so damaging and hurtful." Jim looked down at the phone in his lap, as I drove back to the Priory. Then he tapped it with a forefinger. "I've taken photos of everything, I'll put it on one of Martin's large PCs so that we can all look at it together. I don't know who these people are, but Demelza and Maggie will. There may well be a suspect in amongst this lot."

***

The evening was drawing in, a slight mist hung over the hills in the distance. When we reached the courtyard and got out of the van, the chill of the evening held the aroma of woodsmoke, and the hint of an approaching frost. My cottage door opened, and Flora and Lottie rushed to greet me. Martin followed behind them, grinning at their exuberant greeting towards me.

"I fed them both for you, and of course Cleo," he said as my cat stood beside him disdaining the sloppy greeting the dogs were giving me. A polite dip of her head, the waving tail, and she retreated back into the warmth of the lounge and the window seat. That greeting from Cleo would be all I would get, but it was enough for me.

The cottage was warm, the wood burner was lit and glowing. "Thank you, Martin, I appreciate this and so do the pets." I laughed as both dogs snuggled down in front of the warmth of the log burner.

"Come on both of you, to the Priory kitchen. I don't think Sheila will last much longer, she is bursting with curiosity and excitement. We have all been desperate to hear what you have discovered. When you rang and told us you'd be late we decided to send for a pizza. It should be arriving any moment. Come on, let's go."

***

Martin practically frog marched us out of my cottage and into the Priory kitchen. Maggie handed Jim a whisky and I was given a steaming mug of tea. Jim went into the library with Martin, and they got everything organized for us to view the photographs he had taken in the shed. The pizza delivery had arrived, and we all took our seats in the library with a plateful of pizza on our laps.

"This looks as if we are all at the movies. We are all about to see a show!" Sheila said. She sat perched on her chair, leaning forward in anticipation, her smile radiant with excitement. "And what a show it will be," she added.

It was a real show! The photos slid one by one across the screen. Our smiles faded and even Sheila's excitement waned into horror and disbelief. It seemed that the folk in our village had many secrets, some from their past, some concerning marital affairs, others concerning family relationships, family rows, and disputes over wills and businesses. It was astonishing to find out what lay behind closed doors, and the seemingly normal people with their cheerful smiling faces. Some of the secrets were silly and petty. One neighbour periodically snipped the prize blooms from next door to place bouquets upon graves. Others seemed more serious and malicious, and it was with a dawning realization upon everyone that nothing, and no one in our village could be taken at face value. There was the unspoken thought that after a nights rest, and in the fresh morning light, clarity would come. There would be a breakthrough as we all looked again at the information we had amassed. With solemn faces we adjourned for the night, all of us stunned by our new knowledge about our friends and neighbours.

After breakfast each of us took a mug of coffee, or in my case tea into the library to look again at the photos.

"This is all very well, but who is there in this group who would kill to keep their secret? Someone must have been threatened by the disclosure of their secret to the public. Who stands to lose the most? Whose actual livelihood would be threatened? Whose marriage will collapse? It's a nightmare trying to figure out who would act to keep their secret, and would actually stoop to kill. Can you single anyone out? Who do you think is the most likely suspect?" Jim asked everyone. No one replied, the implications of a killer being a friend or neighbour too great to envisage, let alone talk about.

"You said that the padlock had been tampered with. Someone must have entered that shed before us," I reminded Jim.

"Yes, I think some opened letters had been taken. Roy was obviously methodical, and had an ordered table. But part of that table had empty spaces as if some letters had been removed."

"What does that mean? Why would someone take them?" Sheila asked Jim.

"To continue the blackmail after the murder of Roy. I don't think Roy's death is going to be the end of the blackmail." Jim said, and a fearful silence grew at these words. Into that silence could be heard the heavy footsteps down the kitchen corridor warning us that Tenby was on his way. With a quick movement of the mouse, Martin had changed the PC screen to an innocuous photo of the Priory. Jim gave him an approving smile, and took a place at the large table in front of the library windows. Jim lifted a paper and began making notes. His research on the Knights Templars in the area was ongoing, but it always took second place whenever we had a murder to contend with and solve. Intriguing facts about some families living in the county was a new aspect to his research. It gave him a pretext to be busy when the inspector entered the room.

"Okay Flora, that's enough now." The door opened with a great commotion of dogs bouncing around the inspector. He was a great favorite with all the dogs, but it was Flora who had been his puppy for a few weeks, that loved him to bits. Always she greeted him with a special bark. The large bulk of the inspector would give any criminal pause for thought, and his face could hold a hard shrewd look that brooked no opposition or lies. That same criminal would be astonished if they could see the look of soppy adoration Tenby gave to all the pets. But especially Flora. "I expect the village grapevine has been busy. You've all heard?"

CHAPTER FIFTEEN

At our puzzled looks Tenby rubbed his hands almost gleefully. "Ha, it's good to know that I am the bearer of fresh news. Although its unpleasant news at that. Mrs. Evans has been attacked and is now in a coma. I've come to see Jim and Daisy, I gather you went selling raffle tickets yesterday. Okay, I know why you went. It was a ploy to find out about the blackmailing attempts of Roy Jones." Tenby held up his arm to stop us from speaking. "Yes, you were extremely helpful yesterday finding that shed with all Roy Jones stuff in it. Now I want to know what was said when you went to visit Mrs. Evans. What did she have to say? And was any of it about Roy Jones?"

Jim sent the photos from his phone of the blackmailing letter that he had secretly taken which Mrs. Evans had received to Tenby. Tenby's eyes widened when we told him about her vitriolic remarks and hatred of Roy Jones. But he groaned in dismay when we told him about the secret she had held concerning Roy himself. "I wonder what that secret was. If only she had told someone. Perhaps when she wakes up we'll know who attacked her." He shook his head, and with a quick pat on Flora's head he bustled out of the room.

I said nothing. I looked over Jim's shoulder at the photos of the blackmail letter Mrs. Evans had received. She hadn't been a pleasant woman, but that didn't merit an attempt on her life. I thought back to yesterday, how careful she'd been when she opened the door to us. How delighted she had been to have a good moan about Roy. She'd been hugging the secret of Roy Jones to herself, but she told us that she had it. Who else knew that she had that secret? Did that secret involve someone else who would not have wanted it made public? Was it the secret of Roy Jones that had got her attacked, or was it some other reason?

***

"What now?" Sheila asked, drawing her Agenda book out of her capacious bag. "What about plans for the day? We have one murder and one attempted murder to solve now. But at least they can't blame Mary for this attack. Can they? Mary wasn't involved with Mrs. Evans, was she?"

"Demelza spent the night with Mary. Demelza was worried about her, and insisted that she should stay over with her. It's as well she did so, because not only did she give Mary an alibi, but they also face timed Mary's cousin in Taunton that evening. So, for once Mary is absolutely in the clear," Maggie informed us, to relieved sighs from each of us.

"I'm going into Stonebridge; would you like a lift Daisy? I know you want to take a painting into the art shop, and pick up some more painting equipment, we could go together," Jim said.

It was the first I'd heard of a painting to go to the art shop, and as I had stocked up on painting stuff a few days ago, I didn't need any more. It was a ruse. I realized Jim wanted to go somewhere and wanted me with him. On my entry to the library, I hadn't really looked at him, but now I realized the new lines of worry on his face had deepened.

"That'll be great Jim. Does anybody else need anything from Stonebridge? I'll get Flora and Lottie ready for the puppy class before I go. They are both benefiting from the class and seem to know when it's puppy class day. Going with both of you is great fun, somehow they think it's special to have both Maggie and Martin with them. They are excited even when they get up."

Flora and Lottie sat in the cage in the back of the SUV. Both had been brushed and sat upright with big grins on their puppy faces. They knew it was fun time with all the other puppies.

Jim approached Maggie and Martin as they were about to drive off. "That was a lot of information you both got from the class when we were investigating the puppy farm murder. I know it's not the same, as it's not about puppies. But see if you can get any gossip about Roy Jones this morning. His murder, and now the latest news of Mrs. Evans will surely be the main topic of conversation. That puppy class group comes from all around the area. They may well know something that we wouldn't find out about in the village."

***

Maggie and Martin drove off out of the courtyard under the archway. The frost had not been severe last night, the grip of the winter was slowly lessening, and the sun had broken through early enough to take off the chill. I loved the mornings in Cornwall. The cold freshness of this morning carried with it a faint tang of the sea. Nowhere in Cornwall were you far from the coast. When the wind was in the right direction, the sea could be evident as it swirled about you, carried in moist air across the moorland.

"We'll take my Audi. Remember!" Jim tapped his ear, indicating that his car had been bugged. We both got in the car, and he drove off following the SUV down the lane. "I can't imagine why Mrs. Evans had to be killed. I thought she seemed harmless enough. I know she was friendly with Roy Jones, although that didn't stop him from sending her a blackmailing letter. I keep coming back to that secret she knew about him. Did it concern someone else? And was that the person who attacked her?" The exasperation in Jim's voice sounded as if it was over Mrs. Evans murder. But I knew better. The murders were an interesting puzzle, to be worried over, just like a dog worried over a bone. No, his exasperation was purely over this attack on him, not a physical attack, but one on his privacy. He was worried, but I also felt fear. Our conversation was about ordinary everyday things. It was difficult to talk naturally, knowing that each word you said would be listened to at a later date by someone else.

"This new person, the second blackmailer and Roy's killer must be the one who attacked her. But if she knew about Roy's secret, how would that cause her death? You're right Jim, that secret must include someone else. There must be a link between blackmailer number one Roy Jones, and the second blackmailer, his murderer. This second blackmailer must have known about Roy's blackmailing, and he must have known about the shed for him to steal those steamed letters. There must be a link as I've said already between the two blackmailers." At this remark Jim nodded his head in agreement. "But there must be another link between the two blackmailers and Hilda Evans. Otherwise, there would be no need to kill her."

"If you're right Daisy, and I'm not saying you're wrong, how the hell do we find these links?"

I slumped back in my seat convinced that my theory was correct. I was however in full agreement with Jim. How would we find those links? It seemed an impossible task. Both of us sank back in our seats. There was an air of despondency and frustration in the car. I knew why I was frustrated. But Jim had reached mega levels in the frustration he felt with the murder, and now the Watcher, as I was now calling his unknown foe. Conversation became desultory between us. Neither of us had much to say. Everything had been said and deliberated over in this morning's discussion. All we could do was carry on and look for clues as to the blackmailer's identity. Thoughts were going round and round in my head, all leading nowhere. A few sidelong glances at Jim and I saw a furrowed brow and intent look upon his face. He too was thinking, and thinking hard if that look upon his face was anything to go by.

"The hedgerows are coming back into life," my voice rang out in the car making Jim jump.

He gave a startled glance at me, and then at the hedges we were passing as my remark slid into his consciousness. "Yes, yes, spring has almost arrived."

It was true, fat buds were coming out on many trees, and tiny bright green leaves were beginning to show. "I love Cornwall in the Spring, all freshly washed and ready for summer."

"Freshly washed?"

"Yes, the new leaves, buds and blossom are always so bright and green. Especially in Cornwall, it looks as if they have been freshly washed!"

I'd not expected Jim to love my fanciful expressions, but to my surprise he just grinned at me. "Yes, that's true, especially in Cornwall."

It was almost with a sense of relief that we drew into the car park in Stonebridge. Conversation had been stilted and forced. It had been difficult chatting, knowing that there was a microphone beside you.

We got out of the car. As I struggled to extricate myself from the low-slung passenger seat, I heard a great roar of machinery come to a halt behind me. Looming over me was a large shadowy figure and it was coming closer.

CHAPTER SIXTEEN

I froze. Turning round to look at it was not an option. The large looming shaped towered behind me. My bag and one foot were still in the car. The other was on the ground. Somehow I'd extricated myself from Jim's car in a cack-handed fashion, and was now half in and half out of it. From the corner of my eye that looming black shape, or figure was now right behind me. I felt, rather than saw it make a move towards me. My head seemed to have gone vacant. I didn't even call for help from Jim. The unexpectedness of it froze not only my body but also my brain. Then from the inner depths of my very being, I drew in a deep shuddering breath and acted. My handbag and my art folder were still clutched in my left hand on my lap. I swung them up and rose from my seat putting my weight on my grounded leg. Possessed by an inner unknown strength I swung them up and at the shape. "Get away! Keep away from me!"

I felt the blow from my bag and folder connect with the shape. There was a loud gasp and the shape hurtled backwards with the crash of metal upon the ground, accompanied by loud curses and groans. The curses reached my ears. I closed my eyes, and kept them tight shut. Not only did I recognise the voice, but I knew at once what that tremendous crash of metal had been. If I opened my eyes I knew what I would see. I didn't want to open my eyes; I didn't want to see the awful sight that would meet my gaze. Fearful of what I might see, I slowly turned round to face the devastation I had caused. A large motorbike lay on its side. That was what had caused the crash of metal. A large figure, clad in black leather, and clutching a helmet, was trying to extricate himself from beneath the motorbike. Jim went forward and began pulling the bike upright, and helped the figure to his feet. It was Sam. He had been my erstwhile attacker in our previous escapades, and even now I found it difficult to accept him as a friend. I hadn't realized that it was him. The loud roaring noise behind me, and the figure and bike looming over my shoulder had set off my instinctive reaction. "Sorry Sam, I didn't know it was you." My apology sounded lame even in my ears, and judging by the glare I received from Jim he also thought it pathetic. "I really am sorry. Did I hurt you? Have I damaged your bike?"

Sam's exasperated voice shouted at me, "Daisy! When will you stop attacking me?"

Jim walked round the Audi towards me. He was doubled up, clutching his sides, and laughing so much I was frightened he'd have a heart attack. "Trust you Daisy. The poor chap was trying to be friendly. Did you have to clout him so hard? What have you got in that bag of yours?"

Sam finally rose to his feet, set the bike straight and upright, and dusted himself down. Only after he had carefully checked all over his precious Vincent 1000 Black Shadow. "This time Daisy, both myself and my bike are unhurt. That was some wallop!" He rubbed his jaw, and then grinned at me. "No harm done, but you can at least buy me lunch to make amends."

"Good idea," agreed Jim.

"Okay, I'll pay for lunch, but I was scared when you roared up out of nowhere behind me," I said.

"Don't worry. That message was received. Never ever come up behind Daisy and catch her unawares!" Sam laughed at my still appalled face, and Jim joined in.

I smiled at them. But I really would have loved to have kicked them both. It was with a bad grace I followed them to the hotel for lunch. The last time I had been in that hotel was with my ex-husband. That was the day I had told him in no uncertain terms, that I didn't want to get back with him. Remembering how I had walked out on Nigel, my head held high and my confidence wavering despite my brave face, I found it almost amusing to find myself back here with two other men in my life. Thankfully, there were no romantic entanglements with either of them. I ignored that little voice in my head which muttered, 'what about Jim?'

Our table was in a corner, well away from the other tables giving us privacy. Jim's habitual need to have a corner table and his back to the wall came into play yet again. There were four chairs around the corner table, both Sam and I took the chairs either side of him. Not one of us wished to have our back to the room. What does that say about us, I wondered? Were we beginning to think like Jim? I knew I was. But what about Sam?

The drinks had come, and our orders taken. Sam put his drink down, "I'm doing the painting and finishing off in the stable cottage that will be Gerald's. I'm trying to buy an old blacksmith's cottage and forge, and convert it into a garage to repair and renovate classic motorcycles. To pay for it, both Gerald and I have agreed to sell my father's cottage. It's too big for either one of us, and has a huge garden and outbuildings which we can never keep up with, neither of us having the time nor the love of gardening that dad had. Martin was wondering whether to get a decorator in for the stable cottage, and the last unrenovated apartment in the Priory House. I don't mind painting, or renovating old furniture, it's been a handy way to make money over the years, so we agreed that I would do it. Whilst painting a window at the stable cottage, I saw you Jim. You were busy with a gadget in your car. I knew what you were doing, but I'd love to know why."

Jim sat very still. His hand tightened on his glass, and he stared into the liquid as if there would be answers written there. I said nothing. This was between Sam and Jim. It was up to Jim whether he explained everything to Sam. The question was, did Jim trust Sam? After all, Sam had shot Jim in the leg, and in cold wet weather Jim still limped.

"Yes Sam. You're correct, I was looking for bugs in my car. I found one."

"I thought you did. You stopped suddenly, and I could sense that you were furious from across the courtyard," Sam said with a quiet satisfaction that his surmise had been correct.

"My cottage has been professionally searched, and there are two bugs in place, one downstairs, and one upstairs."

Sam gave a whistle, and looked at Jim. "That's pretty serious. Who do you think has planted the bugs? And why?"

"I don't know. That's the worrying part. I don't know who planted them. I don't know who searched my cottage and I don't know why. There must be a reason, but for the life of me I just cannot find one."

Conversation came to an end when the waitress returned with our meals. I had sat listening whilst this conversation was going on. I was taken aback when Sam looked at me and asked, "any ideas Daisy?"

"No. Personally I think it must be to do with Jim's past life. He's never been the typical civil servant, so maybe…" I didn't know what else to add. How much of his past life did Jim want Sam to know? I felt that it was not my place to explain.

We began eating. I had a Ploughman's whilst the other two had gone for the steak and kidney pie. That pie required concentration and dedication to enjoy every morsel. They were not talking, but I knew they were thinking. It seemed to me that we went round in circles, and that more information was needed before we could come to any conclusion.

Sam put down his knife and fork. "What were you? MI5? Or CIA?"

"Something like that," answered Jim.

"Why did I ever try and tangle with you two? The spy and the Daisy!" Sam shook his head in disbelief.

Jim laughed, the first real laugh that I had had heard for some time. "I don't know who it is, or what they are looking for. I've contacted a couple of friends, they were investigating for me, but they found nothing. But they have other avenues to explore, they might still find something. Whoever it is, they are good. Very good! The equipment they have used is top quality, only available from military suppliers."

"I'm around now each day, I'll keep an eye out for you. I may be able to find out from the other side of the law if you'd like me to try? Don't worry Daisy, I have left it all behind me, but I still have contacts. Shall I ask around Jim?"

Jim looked at Sam. He wanted to say no, he'd have liked to have been able to say there was no need. But Jim was facing an unknown enemy or killer, and it was eating him up. "Okay Sam, I'd appreciate it."

When the meal was finished, we sat back. It seemed strange, the three of us joined together in our search for Jim's unknown enemy. Make no mistake I thought, it had to be an enemy. Why else would his cottage be bugged?

"Where will you live when the cottage is sold? Is your new building habitable?" I asked Sam.

He shook his head, "Martin has kindly said I can stay at the Priory, either in the apartment I'm sorting out for him, or with Gerald."

"Quite an undertaking, opening a business and converting the building. Have you experience in running a motorcycle business like this?" Jim asked Sam.

"Yes, a mate and I had one out in Spain for a while. He bought me out. It's quite successful, and I know all about getting the business started, and then building it up," Sam replied.

Two texts came in for me. One was from Martin telling me about a possible lead in the search for my father. The other was obviously an excited one from my twin sister Violet. *Pick you up from Stonebridge to visit the shop where Martin suggests we look. Ten minutes. Okay?*

I explained that I was about to search for my father. Jim looked at me with concern. "I don't think you're too happy about this. Can you cope with it?" At Sam's puzzled look, Jim explained my newfound 'twin sister' determination to find our father. "Daisy has had a lot of stuff, for want of a better word, going on in her life in the last few months. I don't think more trauma is a good idea."

My bag over my shoulder, I stood at the table, "I don't see any way out, Violet is desperate to find out who her father was. Or rather our father. No Jim, I'm not too happy about it. If he had been an honourable man, surely he would have married our mother. I do wonder if we are going to find out something that would have been better left in the past." I left the hotel and walked to the car park to meet Violet, and possibly my Father.

CHAPTER SEVENTEEN

"Hi Daisy. Isn't this exciting? I wonder what we'll find out? What do you think?" Violet's words tripped off her tongue, as she stood by her car. Her eagerness worried me. I remembered her initial attitude towards me when I approached her about my family history. Our mother's reaction to me, was disbelief and denial of my certificates and documents. My mother accepted me now. Her love for my son Jake had been unconditional and overwhelming. But those few days of rejection still clouded my family reunion. Violet had grown up in a loving family, and never had the feelings that an adopted child has. My adoptive parents, one of whom was my aunt I found out later, had been loving. However, knowing I was adopted had caused me to wonder why my birth mother had given me up. "Violet don't build up your hopes. It may take many months or years to find out who our real father is. Or we may never find him. Please, don't expect too much."

Her face clouded over, and she frowned at me. "Don't you want to find out? Have you no interest in finding out who our father was?"

"Yes, I do have an interest. But I'm also realistic in that I wonder what sort of man leaves his girlfriend pregnant, and disappears from her life." My harsh words were meant in a kindly way, but Violet stiffened and pulled a face at me. She got in the car, and I got into the passenger seat beside her.

Before we drove off, I put my hand on her arm. "Violet, I'm scared. I'll be honest, your mother's initial rejection of me, sorry, our mother's initial rejection of me has made me frightened of what this search will bring. Lately, so much has been going on in my life, I don't think I can face any more upset."

Violet sat still for a moment, hands on the steering wheel. She took a deep breath, and then turned to face me. "Sorry Daisy, I didn't think about all you've been through lately. It must have taken a lot of courage to leave your marriage, your home and start a new life down in Cornwall. You always seem so capable, and never seem to show any fear or distress. I never thought that underneath you're struggling with all the changes in your life." With an impulsive move she bent forward, and gave me a hug. "Don't worry, I really think this will go well, eventually. But I'll take your advice, and not build my hopes up. I'll take each day as it comes in our search. Promise!"

Why? Why did suddenly tears come to my eyes? Before I knew what had happened, tears ran down my cheeks. "Thanks Violet," I whispered, and squeezed her arm in recognition of her words, and of how we had found a way forward in our search, together.

The car jerked forward. Violet was an atrocious driver, and I checked that my seatbelt was safely secured. Surreptitiously I placed a hand on the seat, gripping it hard for fear of bumps, scrapes and outright accidents. "It's only a small shop, it's now selling bric-a-brac and kitchenalia. I think it used to be a small general store. Martin reckons one of the chaps in the photo lived here and ran it for many years. He thinks that a daughter has now taken the shop on, and is running it now with the bric-a-brac in place of the general store."

***

Violet parked outside, and we both got out of the car. Violet had a photocopy of the group photograph. The shop window displayed an eclectic mix of old-fashioned kitchen gadgets, trendy pottery and an abundance of dried flowers everywhere. Violet pushed the door open. A large bell clanged above our heads, making us both jump. A harassed looking woman came out of the back room. "Can I help you?" At first glance she didn't look as if she wanted to help us at all. But then a weak smile was plastered on her face as she walked forward, whilst casting an anxious look behind her.

I picked up a small basket, handwoven with a pretty, intricate pattern. "I like this, I'll take this please." Violet, now aware of my maneuvers into a pleasant conversation with the woman, before starting on our family history search, followed my lead.

An earthenware pot held a display of dried flowers, complete with tiny fir cones and grasses. "This is delightful, I must have this," said Violet carrying it towards the counter. Our purchases were wrapped and placed into paper bags, with a meaningless conversation about the weather. A glance towards me from Violet, and I began speaking about the real purpose of our visit. "I'm sorry to bother you, but we found an old photograph in our mother's possessions. She seems to think that the gentleman on the left was the owner of this shop. Can that be right?" I saw out of the corner of my eye, the nod of approval from my sister, at this way of asking the question, the burning question of why we'd come.

The woman took the photocopy, her dark hair fell forward, and the faded blouse and worn jeans seemed highlighted, as a stray sunshine beam glanced in the window across the shop. She brushed the hair back with one hand, and continued to stare at the photograph. "My father has come into the shop today. He's sitting in the back room, I'll call him, and he'll tell you himself."

A few minutes later the old man appeared, grumbling at being summoned from an armchair and his television viewing. When the door was pushed wider as he walked through it, the sports announcer's voice echoed around the shop. Told of the purpose of our visit, he was shown the photocopy. At the information that we were the daughters of one of the women he scrutinized us, and then the photocopy of our mother. "You look like her, when she was young that is. Just like her, both of you. Don't expect she looks like that now! Like me, she'll be old and decrepit." The photocopy was studied, held away from him in the silence that crept over us all in the shop. "Yes that's me. That photograph was taken by your mother." He told the woman beside him. "We were just engaged when she took it."

The disappointment that Violet felt was obvious in her sigh beside me. "Can you tell me anything more about the other people in the photograph? Any information about the people in this photograph would be of great help to us." He gave us the names of each person. Violet wrote them down in a notebook, whilst I with coaxing and listening to tales of the past years, managed to add a little further information to the photocopy. The other young woman had passed away some years ago after moving to Manchester. The old man seemed to consider that the move to Manchester had been the fatal instrument of her demise. My sister's impatience at the story of the woman was obvious to me, but I could only hope that the old man wasn't conscious of it. Whilst he did tell us the names of the three other men, he'd only met them that day, and couldn't remember much information about them. In his defense it had been his first and only meeting with them. Thanking them both, we clutched our purchases and went to the car.

***

"That's not too bad. So lucky having him there today, and

remembering the stuff he did. That's three names we have now to give to Martin and Sheila. Perhaps there will be further information on the Internet that they can find out about them. He was all right that old boy, but I'm glad he wasn't our father, aren't you?" I asked Violet.

"Yes, I think I am. If he had been our father, she might well have been our half-sister. He was a bit cranky, wasn't he? Do you know Daisy, I'm beginning to see what you mean about this family history business? I think I'm going to be more circumspect in future. After all, our dad could be a criminal, or a thief or…," Words failed her, and Violet spluttered to a stop.

"Yes, we can have a choice. If we don't like the sound of our dad, we don't even need to acknowledge him. We could have a five-point plan, that only suitable dad's fitting our plan would be accepted into our family. Violet, we can pick and choose. If we decide that we don't want him as our father, we needn't approach him and can just get on with our lives without him."

"You make it sound like we'll pick and mix, Daisy. Only the best will do, all mediocre or horrible types, need not apply." Violet gave a snort, and rested her head on the steering wheel shaking with laughter. I joined in the laughter, and when we both recovered, she drove off, still smiling.

***

Violet dropped me off at the Priory. She had to get back to Sheba, and I felt Martin had looked after my pets for long enough. And I was tired. Violet and I were the same age, but sometimes I felt she had more energy than I did. Then I thought to myself, she lived alone with Sheba, and her routine was the same every day, and had been for years. My life consisted of constant daily upheavals whilst living in a disaster zone.

I walked across the courtyard towards my cottage. Jim must've been looking out for me, because as I reached my front door he came out of his cottage. "Are you all right Daisy? How did it go?"

CHAPTER EIGHTEEN

"Come in and I'll tell you. He wasn't our father. Thank goodness, neither of us liked him. We are going to be careful before we introduce ourselves, in case we don't like our prospective father. We now have a five-point plan before we accept anyone as our father." I began to laugh, "Violet was actually appalled that he might've been our father."

There was relief in Jim's face, and he began to smile and followed me inside. After the initial greeting from the pets, I went towards the kitchen area and put on the kettle. Jim followed me, his face becoming grave. "Whilst I was out, someone has been at my cottage, and placed cameras around it now! I think I'd better check your cottage Daisy!" Jim checked the outside the front of my cottage, then inside. He then went through to the back of the cottage, and outside my kitchen window and door. Shaking his head, he said, "all clear."

"Have you any cameras inside the house, are they just outside?" I asked him.

"One outside the cottage. It's been so cleverly sited; you'd hardly see it. The sun caused it to glint as I walked up to the front door, otherwise I would never have spotted it. I immediately checked inside, but that was the only one in the front, and one beside the gate, and near my back door." Taking a seat, again he shook his head. "Why? What do they expect to see?? I can only think that writing my memoirs has caused this attempt to see what I'm doing. But I can't understand how anyone would know what I was doing. I've never mentioned it even to you, so how would anyone know that I have started the book? I wouldn't put anything in that was secret, or about anyone else that could put them in danger. I signed the

Official Secrets Act. This book was going to be a generalized account of my visits to different countries, and the customs I found there that were of interest. I didn't expect to publish it. As you know I have a son out in New Zealand, with a couple of young boys. His wife and I didn't get on, so we don't have that much contact. But I thought it would be interesting to have this story, an account of my life if ever my grandsons were interested in my past history."

"What will you do? Remove the cameras or leave them?" I said, and handed him a mug of coffee.

"I've been thinking about that. I think I had best leave them alone. Somehow I'll try to get some of mine up now without them noticing."

This was getting complicated, but I said nothing. What could I say? Now I knew! He had signed the official secrets act. He had been in some sort of secret occupation. This memoir of his was possibly a worrying object to somebody. What were they frightened of? What had he done in his past to initiate this fear? Why these precautions to find out what Jim was doing now? I was worried for him. Also, I was worried for the rest of us. Someone with the know-how and the financial clout to install these highly expensive pieces of spyware was not your average burglar. This was far more serious, and I began to understand why Jim was so worried. To take his mind off it all, I told him about the latest in our father search. He laughed as I explained again Violet's dislike of the old man, and our five-point plan. "I think that Violet will want to vet anyone we think is a possibility, before we approach them." I told Jim.

"That's not a bad idea. We all have relatives that we don't like, and wouldn't want to own them." Jim said and grinned at my face.

***

After our evening meal, we adjourned to the library with coffee. Maggie had received a phone call during the meal, taking it outside the kitchen. On her return I noticed the serious look on her face and had wondered what was wrong.

"As you know I had a phone call during the meal. It was Demelza, she's just been for emergency treatment, and she's asked if she can stay with me tonight. She wants me to let you know what's going on. Her ex-husband is out of jail, and he's been stalking her yet again. He caught up with her tonight, so hopefully the police will get onto him. But it's doubtful, because he said he has an alibi. He's got some friends to vouch for him. They always do. The bastard gave her that scar on her face." There was an outbreak of comments, swearing and general disgust at the thought of our Demelza being attacked in this way.

"We've done nothing to collect more information on the murder and the attack," said Sheila. Her face mirrored her disappointment at the lack of evidence that we had found. "It's been boring, no fun at all. There hasn't been a car chase, an explosion or…"

"There have been nearly two murders," Jim protested.

"Actually, we do seem to have ground to a halt, I agree with Sheila," said Martin.

"We can't keep selling raffle tickets door to door, nor can we break into village cottages one by one," an exasperated Jim added.

"What can we do?" Sheila demanded looking around the group. "There must be something more we can do to help Mary. We can't just leave it at this. And we must sort out this stalker of our Demelza!"

"Tomorrow. Let's sleep on it tonight. We'll sort

84

something out tomorrow, and get organized then," I said to general agreement.

***

I was tired that night, and went to bed eager for sleep. As is the usual case, sleep didn't come. I read for a while, watched some TV, but in the end got myself a cup of tea and listened in the semidarkness to a favorite audiobook. It was Flora's low growl deep in her throat that first alerted me. A slight movement could be heard from outside in the courtyard. I threw on my dressing gown, and crept over to the window lifting a corner of the blind. Yes, there was definite movement on the opposite side of the courtyard. Grabbing my phone I texted Jim, *Intruder in courtyard*. The dogs by this time were alert and beside me. Flora's low growl was echoed by Lottie. "Stay there, be quiet and be good," I told them and crept towards my front door. The text came back from Jim, *Okay, on it, stay put.*

The window seat in my lounge held a hidden compartment, I reached inside it and produced a weapon, one from my secret stash of weapons — eBay was a great place for interesting stuff!

***

Clutching it in both hands I crept out of my front door. Jim was already out, and I could see him in the faint moonlight in the courtyard. The other figure that had alerted me, was fiddling with the door leading into the empty stable cottage. Jim approached him, I was amazed at how quiet he was, he literally crept up on him without a sound. But the figure crouched over the door must've had a sixth sense. Whirling around he tackled Jim and flung him to the ground. Jim fell back onto the cobblestones, and the figure made as if to attack him yet again.

"Oh no you don't!" I cried out and dashed across the courtyard with my gun pointing at the intruder.

CHAPTER NINETEEN

My dressing gown swung out behind me. I readied my gun like my favourite cops did on TV. "Leave him alone! Take that!" I pressed the trigger on my gun, and closed my eyes. It was a direct hit on the intruder in the middle of his chest. I drew closer to the struggling men. Jim lay flat on his back, and the intruder had begun to rise to his feet. But my pepper spray had caused the intruder to rear back, before gasping and falling to his knees clutching his eyes and face. Jim rolled over and covered his face before the spray reached him. Some of it did. Lights flared out over the courtyard, and Martin raced out of his cottage with a large flashlight in his hand. Jim and I shielded our eyes from the bright glare, but the intruder was still too busy trying to cope with the pepper in his face.

The illuminated scene before us showed in sharp relief the two figures. No longer shadowy outlines they were obviously two men, one of whom was Jim as I already knew. It was the other figure still clawing at his face that I also recognized. "Oh no! Oh no, not again!" I sighed, and dropped my pepper spray gun to my side, and then behind my back.

Jim had also seen his assailant and he too was puzzled, horrified, and for once lost for words. The lights in the Priory kitchen came on, and the two figures of Maggie and Demelza rushed out towards us. By the time they reached us Jim and Martin were helping my latest victim to his feet.

"What's happened here?" shouted Maggie she rushed towards us.

"It's Daisy yet again! She's pepper sprayed Sam." Jim's reply was shouted back. It echoed loudly around the courtyard. A most unhelpful reply I thought, and completely without the extenuating circumstances that my action had warranted.

"It's Jim's fault. I told him there was an intruder." I snapped back at Jim. "He told me he was going to stop him. I rushed out and found him struggling with a large man. I saw Jim fall to the ground and of course went his rescue. Why were you attacking Sam?" I demanded of Jim.

"For goodness sake, stop talking and let's get Sam into the kitchen and those eyes bathed immediately. He's in a terrible way," said Maggie.

"Why have you got a pepper spray gun?" Martin asked me.

"Because Jim said a Taser gun was illegal, otherwise I'd have had one of them!"

"Does that mean I have to be thankful to you Jim? But for you I would have been tasered instead of pepper sprayed?" Sam snuffled through his hands.

***

We all trooped into the kitchen. Everyone was disheveled and in nightwear, except for Sam. I eyed him with suspicion, and I noticed Jim was also looking him up and down, once he'd finished wiping his eyes again. There had been a slight cloud of pepper spray that had also reached Jim and inflamed his eyes. My dressing gown was large with huge patch pockets, quilted and in a bright red satin. It was pretty eye-catching. The pockets thankfully were so big that my gun had slid easily into one. I acted quickly, so removing the embarrassing evidence of yet another mishap. I saw Demelza look at my dressing gown in amazement. It had been a present to me from my son and future daughter-in-law. They had bought it for me on a stopover in Singapore. I wondered what Demelza would say when I turned round. There was a huge Dragon climbing up the back!

"Why were you at that doorway Sam? What were you doing? I thought you were a burglar," said Jim. He was sitting down at the table, the pepper spray, the little he had, had cleared from his eyes and face. His navy-blue dressing gown was still neat, after he had brushed all the courtyard dust from it.

The kettle was boiling for my tea. The whisky bottle stood on the counter beside the coffeepot burbling away, alongside swabs of pepper-stained cotton wool and antiseptic cream.

"Well, the app works on our phones," I said brightly, hoping to break the sullen silence that hung over the men. Our intruder Sam was still mopping his eyes and face from my pepper spray attack. The app on each phone newly installed by Martin, had six screens. This showed areas of the courtyard, and the Priory kitchen door and outside the archway. Each screen could be brought up and enlarged, highlighting any intruder. This is what I had done. Contacting Jim as I had been told to do, was also the correct procedure. Was it my stupidity that he dashed out without a light? I don't think so! Was it my fault that he moved around when fighting Sam, and caught some of the pepper spray blast? Judging by that look on his face he obviously thought it was.

"What were you doing at that time in the morning at the stables Sam?" Tenby asked when he joined us in the kitchen.

Thank goodness, someone asking a sensible question I thought, pouring the boiling water onto my teabag. The others were all sitting with whisky, and in Sam's case I thought a second one would be required.

"I wanted to get a piece of furniture finished," Sam muttered, placing the wet pepper-stained cloth down, and reaching for his whisky glass. "Oh hell, you might as well know." A large swallow of whisky was followed by a sigh of satisfaction. "I was hoping to buy a cottage and old Forge, and set up a motorbike repair garage with input from a mate. We got a buyer for dad's cottage, ready to exchange tomorrow. This afternoon I heard I'd been gazumped out of the old Forge, and now my mate says that he was too busy to come in with me anyway."

"What will you do now?" Jim asked cutting through the commiserations from all of us on Sam's ill fortune.

"Daisy and Violet went to the kitchenalia shop the other day." I nodded agreement at this, but wondered where it was leading. "When we cleared out dad's place we found a lot of old kitchen stuff, so I took it over there, hoping to offload it. When I was there I saw some of the furniture he was selling. The restored furniture was badly polished, and the renovated was even worse. I told him I could do better. The old guy asked me to bring in some and he would sell it for me. That's what I was doing. Finishing the furniture whilst trying to work out what I was going to do next."

Jim rose to his feet. "Okay, let's see this furniture."

Surprised at the request, nevertheless Sam took out his key and also rose to his feet. I looked at Tenby who gave me a grin. "Coming Daisy? We'll all protect Sam from any other attacks you might make on him!"

***

Trooping across the courtyard, all in night attire except for Sam, we soon entered the two unconverted stables. The faint aroma of horses and hay still lingered in the building. The wooden partitions of the stalls were still in place. Brick walls, iron hooks and shelves, empty now, had obviously held horsey clobber and still decorated the walls. There were three pieces of furniture and a long table at one end of the large space. The table held the painting stuff Sam was using for the redecoration of the apartments, and the newly refurbished cottage. Surprised by the efficient placing and neatness of the tools, I then turned my attention to the furniture itself.

"This is superb! Fantastic workmanship." Both Jim and Tenby were enthusing over a mahogany chest polished to perfection. I stared at a kitchen cupboard. A pale sage green, it was beautifully painted, and had unusual porcelain handles on the drawers and cupboard doors. Sam produced the photos of the furniture in their original state.

"They were in a shocking mess. You've worked wonders on them Sam. Why are you bothering about motorbikes when you can produce work like this? There is no need for you to spend money on a property and garage. You could do this furniture restoration in your own cottage and its outbuildings!" I told him.

It was a bizarre situation. The gloom of the stables was lit only by swinging bare bulbs hanging from the wooden rafters. Shadows seemed to move behind the wooden partitions as the bulbs swayed in currents of air. Jim and Sam both sported bruises, and each had a burgeoning black eye. The red rimmed eyes clashed with the bluish bruises, and their noses showed the constant wiping from the effects of my pepper spray. Tenby stood staring at me; a huge shaggy brown dressing gown tied tightly around his ample paunch. His ruffled grey and black hair, and stubble added to the bearlike appearance.

Only Sam looked at ease and even looked the part in that setting. He could have ridden in moments before, and stabled his horse in the far corner in the stable. Dark blue jeans, leather boots, and wearing a leather waistcoat over the pale blue denim shirt, he actually looked like a cowboy. "You all think that this work is good enough?" Our tough guy's voice held an unexpected shyness and trepidation at what our answers might be.

"Yes!" were the emphatic answers from every one of us.

"Does your dad's cottage have enough outbuildings," I asked Sam. "Could you use the cottage and the outbuildings as a furniture restoration base? Start up the business selling to that old guy's shop, and even online. There's no need to go and buy further properties, you'd have everything ready at hand."

Silence. Everyone stared at me open mouthed.

"What?" I blurted out, taken aback by the obvious shock at my remarks.

"Brilliant idea Daisy!" Of course, it had to be Jim who found his voice first.

"Sam, if you don't exchange, you have everything you need to get going in the business where you live now. You could start tomorrow!" said Tenby, gesturing towards the finished pieces of furniture.

"Daisy!" Sam rushed towards me and before I could move, he had lifted me up and swung me around. "Daisy, that's a fantastic idea! And no expenditure needed. Gerald will be delighted, he didn't want to sell the cottage, as he's always known it as our home. This way I can get it to work for us both, and get my new business going with very little expenditure. Thank you Daisy!" Sam set me down on the ground, gave me a smacking kiss, and then grinned round at us all. "I won't like breaking the news to the prospective buyer, but I can't become homeless to please them."

We all moved towards the stable door, each one of us yawning. Late hours at our age took it out of us.

"Good night all. To think that I came here depressed at the collapse of my garage plans. I had a fight with Jim, got pepper sprayed by Daisy. Now I'm going home happy, and full of plans for my new furniture restoration business." Sam put on his helmet and got on his motorbike. His grin was so wide that even in the poor light in the courtyard it shone towards us. His farewell cheerful wave made us all smile at his retreating back.

CHAPTER TWENTY

At breakfast next morning Jim's face showed that he had been in a fight. His red rimmed eyes from the pepper spray had gone, but a dark bruise on the side of his face included a black eye. Sheila was furious and accused us of leaving her out of all the fun. The expression on Jim's face mingled with his wounds, and showed that he didn't think it had been fun. Explanations were given and exclaimed over, and we sat back mugs in hand.

Gerald had arrived full of grateful thanks to me, with a broad smile. "Never wanted to have the cottage sold, the cottage has been in the family for generations. Sam is full of ideas for this new venture. Today, he's going to sort out the legal stuff from his attempt to buy the old Forge, and to disappoint the cottage buyers. We feel bad about those people, but there's nothing we can do. Then he's going to see that old guy again at Kitchenalia."

The conversation went around to the weather, and whether this spring would ever start to arrive properly. We were interrupted by the noisy arrival of the post van into the courtyard.

"I don't know this guy, he's new to this round," said Maggie. "I'd better go. He's coming to the Priory kitchen door with loads of mail." She hurried off down the corridor, and we heard voices. Maggie's voice was becoming raised. Looks were exchanged between us, but it was Gerald who rose to his feet and rushed down to the back door. Moments later a red-faced Maggie returned with a large amount of mail in her arms. Gerald followed behind with even more mail, and a few parcels. "I've to put a basket or box at the back door now. Luke refuses to deliver to each cottage and will only deliver everything to the Priory. You've all to pick up your mail here. He was really rude about it, unpleasant and very officious!" Maggie said, dumping the post onto the table.

"That's okay by me, not as convenient but there's no sense in antagonizing the guy," said Jim.

"My pets will be cross though. They love the letters coming through the letterbox, it's the highlight of their morning," I said.

"Some books I ordered," exclaimed a delighted Jim.

I sat looking at the box Gerald had placed on the table beside me. A square box with my name printed in bright green capital letters. Maggie saw me looking at it, "an early Easter egg," she joked.

"I haven't ordered anything. Can't think what it is." I said and slid my knife under the taped ends. A box was beneath the brown paper wrapping. I lifted the lid. The stench was overpowering. My chair fell back with a crash onto the stone floor as I jumped to my feet.

"What the hell?" Jim rushed to my side, the others peering over the table to see what was inside the box giving off that ghastly smell.

A dead goldfish lay on some kitchen paper. A note lay beside it. *I will expose your secret if you don't place £300 in the movable stone beside the bench in the shop car park at 3 o'clock tomorrow. If you don't pay, I will expose your secret and if you tell anybody you will sleep with the fishes!*

"What does it mean?" I blurted out in a state of utter incomprehension. What was this box with a dead goldfish in it being sent to me?

Jim had pulled me back from the table, and was already on his phone. "Tenby? Daisy has had a blackmail letter. In a box with a dead fish! Someone else has taken over from Roy Jones. It comes with the most bizarre statement and is all printed in bright green ink."

***

It was decided that the parcel, wrapping, and the dead body of the poor goldfish would be put in the back kitchen. The door was firmly closed against the smell. Tenby and some poor soul would have to investigate that lot. A fresh pot of coffee was put on, a mug of tea for me, and we all went into the library. The aroma still hung around the kitchen. This required more thought and discussion. It was certainly an unexpected and new development in the blackmail fiasco. All I could think of was why me? What secret had I got to be exposed? "Why the fish? What does that mean?" I asked Jim.

"The Mafia, especially in the 1940s sent a dead fish when they wanted something from that person. It could be money, silence about a murder or whatever, but the dead fish meant that if they disobeyed, they would be murdered, and they would join the fish at the bottom of the sea or a river," Jim replied.

Into the silence that fell as we all digested Jim's words; Sheila looked across at me. "Daisy, if you don't think it's prying…" she began, and then stopped.

By this time, we had all settled down in the library carrying our mugs, with Gerald helping Maggie with toast and cereal with which to help ourselves. No one wished to eat anything else in the kitchen with the remaining lingering stench of the dead fish.

"Sheila, it's not prying, I know you'd all like to know what secrets I have. But I don't know!" I threw out my hands in despair. "I've been thinking and thinking. I don't know what it could be. I don't have any secrets to worry about, or to pay somebody to keep them quiet."

"The note said expose," Jim looked at me, a puzzled look on his face. "Expose, does that mean anything? The information must have come from a letter. A letter that has been steamed open."

"Expose! Of course! Now I recognize it. It was in a note from Jeff. He said he thought it was time to expose me, and he was going to do it himself if I didn't agree to his terms."

They were horrified gasps from each of them. "Jeff the Art shop man? Expose you? What did he mean?" Maggie's voice held a note of real concern.

I laughed at their faces. "Don't worry, it's nothing serious. Jeff has been selling my paintings. I always sign with my initials in a cartouche. I like to hide behind my initials. Jeff reckons that he will sell more of my paintings with my photo, my name, and a few comments about me. That's what his exposition of me was all about."

There was a sigh of relief from all of them. Jim said, "whoever read that letter, completely misunderstood and thought you were being threatened. They thought they could add even more of a threat."

Tenby had gone. We had caught him before he left for work. He had come immediately to take the parcel, its wrapping paper with the bright green ink and the poor dead goldfish.

"That poor goldfish, I wonder where it came from? I hope it was nobody's treasured pet," mourned Sheila.

"I wonder if it came from the empty house outside the village. It has a huge goldfish pond, and a young boy continues to feed them whilst it's up for sale. An old lady lived there. She recently died, and her three children are still fighting over the will. That is why it's still empty and still on the market. That's the only goldfish pond I know of," said Maggie.

"You say it's empty Maggie?" Jim said in a soft voice. I looked at him with suspicion. That soft voice of his meant that he was planning something. He caught my enquiring look, and he nodded. "Yes Daisy, I think we ought to have a look there, don't you? Perhaps a stakeout?"

"You mean we should sit and watch for the guy to come back and get another goldfish? That's a daft idea. What if he doesn't come back? I think it's more important for me to decide what I do about this blackmail attempt. I know Tenby says he will get back to me, but surely I should have some say in what is going to happen?" I said.

"Leave that discussion to when Tenby returns," said Sheila. Bouncing on her chair with excitement she said, "I think we should plan a stakeout. That's a great idea of Jim's. We could catch the guy red-handed, or perhaps that should be gold handed!" She chortled and looked round at us with delight. "Get it? Gold handed from the goldfish?"

We all smiled back at her remark, but it was a very weak one from me.

"Did you say the property was for sale Maggie?" Jim asked her.

"There was talk of it being on the market, but it was on the downlow, not advertised at all," she replied.

"Jasper!" Both Jim and I said in unison. On a previous investigation we had visited several properties for sale with Jasper, the estate agent. I had pretended that we were looking for my niece who was trying to move to the area.

"You call him," said Jim. "I'm sure he'd rather hear from you. I made a bad impression on him when I kept banging on walls and poking into cupboards. That was when I was looking for a hidden body."

"He thought you were crazy," I said bluntly, relishing Jim's discomfiture.

"Well, we did find a body there," Jim replied.

"We are looking for goldfish this time, not dead bodies!" I said firmly and got out my phone. As I did so I caught a gleeful expression on Sheila's face.

"What? What's so funny?" I demanded.

"You always say you will find no bodies. But you always do find one!" Sheila laughed.

I gave her a glare, and phoned Jasper. When I put the phone down the others looked at me questioningly. "No, it's not Jasper. He no longer works there; he's moved to the Exeter branch. It's a girl called Frankie. We have an appointment to view in an hour."

CHAPTER TWENTY-ONE

Jim and I arrived outside the unkempt house, which sat in woods beside a river. It was a small river, deep in a valley which added to the gloomy atmosphere. A tall leggy blonde exited from the estate agent car. Its logo was plastered along the side of the car. As I looked at the estate agent's logo, I realised that she was staring at my van. It had just been washed, and the sign along it proclaiming BURT'S BEEFY BANGERS with a rather plump gentleman holding aloft a sausage shone brightly in the sunshine. She swallowed hard, and stuck out her hand as she approached us.

"The house is in a dreadful state, with the garden completely overgrown. But it can't disguise the wonderful potential of both the property and its land. Fabulous position with the garden sloping down to the river, with the wonderful sound of the rippling water." She flung her arms wide encompassing the tall trees and the sad looking house.

"That's if the river doesn't flood," was the sour grumble from Jim behind me.

"Is it properly on the market now?" I asked her.

"Only for keen buyers, it's being kept quiet." Frankie opened the front door as she spoke, and ushered us inside. We walked into a front hall. Stale musty air gathered itself together and flung itself at us. Furniture sat in the rooms through the open doors heavy with blankets of dust. A newspaper lay beside a recliner chair, with the remote control on top of it, the chair near to the television. Then we went into the kitchen. We all stood there horrified.

"Oh no! I haven't been in here before. The owners, siblings who inherited it when their father died, have been arguing over the will. They were supposed to clear it all out and get it ready for sale. This is just terrible! I'm going to ring the office." She rushed down the hall, and we could hear her angry shouts down her phone.

After a moment Jim glanced round the room, then walked to the window to look out at the garden. I was transfixed at the sight of that kitchen table. A solitary place had been laid on the table. One bottle of tomato ketchup sat beside a salt cellar. The owner obviously didn't like pepper. A side plate still had a slice of mouldy bread-and-butter on it. The half-drunk mug of tea showed the urgency and suddenness of the former owners death. I turned on my heel and fled down the hall out into the sunshine beside Frankie. "That's it!" I said to Frankie. "Sorry, but I'm going," and I dashed to the sanctuary of my van.

I watched Jim follow me out of the front door and exchange a few words with Frankie. He walked over to my window. "You okay?" Jim said.

"No! That poor person had been taken ill whilst having his solitary meal." My voice shook, I was near to tears. It had been horrifying in its harsh reality of the suddenness of the man's demise.

"Yes, that side gate will pose no problems if we return tonight to keep watch," he said as he straightened up, not listening to a word I said.

Frankie had finished speaking on the phone and ran up to the van. She looked near to tears. "Please come and look at the garden. I understand that you don't want to go back into the house, I don't either! But I want a promotion, I want to join Jasper in Exeter. He loves it there and has even bought his own house. I'm trying to get money for a deposit, and if I do well in my job here I can join the agency in Exeter. I hate living here with my Gran. Please do come and look at the garden. Then I can say that I showed you the massive potential of the fabulous gardens leading down to the river."

Both Jim and Frankie stared at me with anxious expressions. Both of them wanted me to go down to the garden, but they each had very different reasons. "Okay why not? As long as I don't have to go back into the house," I said. What could go wrong wandering down the garden path towards the river?

Brambles and ivy fought with each other to impede our path. Broken concrete and ancient crazy paving paths laid beside the cottage itself led down to the small river at the bottom of the garden. Half dug holes lay beside the path down beside the river. Some had been there for a while; the weeds were growing tall in them. "They were trying to build a jetty and a store for kayaks and canoes," said Frankie looking at her notes.

Jim proceeding in front of me stiffened and stood, very like a pointer dog sniffing out a scent. "That's the pond isn't it? It's quite a big one," he said.

I looked over his shoulder and could see the pond edged with stones and a rather rickety bench beside it. The bushes and trees loomed over it. Frankie was beside me. At Jim's remark she dashed forward to stand beside the pond pointing into it. "Look there are a few waterlilies, and goldfish swimming about in the water." We circled around the pond, exclaiming over the number of goldfish and the size of them. Frankie began to lead the way back up towards the house. I was following close behind. A clump of nettles in my way made me veer off to the right onto the edge of a newly dug hole.

Frankie was ahead of me, and turned back towards me when I exclaimed in pain. My weak ankle had turned beneath me, and I fell forward onto the edge of the hole. Frankie jumped into the hole and put her arms out to catch me as I fell. I thought it was very kind of her, and was grateful for her speedy movement to come to my aid. But a few moments later I was thinking of that saying, *no good deed goes unpunished.* That certainly applied to Frankie when I fell onto the ground on the edge of the hole. My hands were outstretched, they landed flat on the earth. Perhaps this hole was going to be a foundation for the kayak store I thought. To my astonishment, the earth around the edge of the hole was crumbling beneath my hands.

"Oh no! This ground is collapsing," I cried out. When the full weight of my body landed, I sank into the softened earth. My hands scrabbled to gain a grip on the earth. They didn't. The earth beneath me started to move forward, and crumbs of dirt fell into the hole.

Frankie stretched out her arms. "Take my hand, I'll catch you," she said. Those crumbs of earth gathered momentum and growth. An avalanche of clods of earth descended with a gathering speed into the hole. Frankie stepped back, but she was too late to jump out. Horrified, she flattened herself back against the wall of the excavation. The ground that I lay upon gave a convulsive jerk, and beneath me a large object slid forward into the hole.

CHAPTER TWENTY-TWO

The first thing to appear was a hand, with a stiffened finger pointing. The hand was joined to an arm which gradually emerged from the mix of earth, pushing the pointing finger straight into Frankie's face. Enormous clods of earth showered down around the stricken girl, and then a shoulder and head appeared. The head was twisted to one side, with the eyes glaring fixedly into Frankie's face. That hand finally came to rest upon her shoulder, the face almost at her nose. Her screams echoed round and round the valley. The previously silent birds rose screaming and squawking in aggrieved flight.

Jim grabbed Frankie's arm. "Come on now, out of it!" Her screams became convulsing sobs, and she grabbed at his proffered arm gratefully and clambered out.

I pulled myself back slowly from the edge of the hole. One step after another careful step, I slowly retraced my frightening slide on the soft earth. I'd no wish to repeat that sickening sliding feeling, and I definitely had no wish to join the body now resting in the hole.

"Frankie, take a deep breath, try to calm down," Jim's voice was flustered as he tried to calm the hysterical girl. He cast a pleading look towards me. I brushed down my trousers, seeking to get rid of the worst of the soil, and made my way over towards them. It was difficult clambering over the displaced clods of earth. But I finally reached them and putting my arm around the hysterical girl I led her away. Jim's hand on my shoulder stopped me. "Are you all right Daisy?" His eyes searched my face, and at my nod he seemed reassured.

"I'll see to Frankie. We'll go back to the cars. You'll have to phone Tenby, again!" Whilst I soothed the girl, guiding her back up those broken paths, past the house and out to the road my mind was whirling. Not about the poor dead man. It should have been, I was shocked and saddened at his appearance. No doubt about that! But no, my immediate worry was Tenby's reaction. I could hear his voice. "Daisy's found yet another body!" Perhaps I could put the blame for this one on Frankie?

***

We had reached my van, and her company car. "Let's brush this dirt off our clothes and sit in the cars." I brushed frantically at my trousers and jacket. The horrid thought that ran into my brain was that the earth could have been from beside the dead man. I didn't mention that thought to Frankie.

"I'll sit in your van. It won't matter if that gets dirty, not like my company car." Frankie said she continued to brush her clothes furiously.

I swallowed the retort that rose to my mind, and opened the door to the passenger seat. Jim had now joined us, having phoned the police. He began pacing up and down the lane. What was it with Jim and this pacing business I thought? It's becoming a habit to him in times of crisis. Couldn't he bite his nails or…"

Frankie's wailing interrupted my thoughts. "I'll never get that promotion now! I'll be stuck here forever. I can't bear living here on Bodmin Moor. I want to be independent; I don't want to live with my Gran. Why did this have to happen to me?" Her brown eyes stared into mine, drowned in tears they may be, but still they glowed with a beautiful luminosity. Her hair was a shiny bob, she only had to shake it and it fell back into place. A quick brush down of her elegant pantsuit, and she looked fresh and ready for estate agent action.

I on the other hand, still had the dirt clinging to me, no

matter how hard I tried to rub it off. My hair I knew was sticking out in all directions. And all I could smell was that dead body aroma, that had engulfed me when he'd slid from beneath me into the hole.

The police car came speeding down the lane. I shrank back into my seat as I saw Tenby's thunderous look. Oh no! I'll get the usual snide remarks about finding dead bodies. Hell! Nothing could be further from my mind when investigating. I didn't want to find any bodies! Anyway, it could be said that Frankie and Jim were as much to blame as I was. All three of us had found this one, not just me

"Was it a man?" Frankie's whisper came beside me. "I closed my eyes after the hand came towards me."

"Yes, it was an older man with grey hair. It was the grumpy old postman who took over Roy Jones round. Luke something. That's all I noticed, but it was enough. He was very dead, and I didn't want to look any more," was my reply.

Tenby strode up to the van. "Do you realise that the murder statistics of Bodmin Moor are off the charts since you arrived? Why don't you stay at home Daisy? Oh no, that doesn't work either, you have bodies delivered to your door!"

I looked away from him quickly, his unexpected asperity had brought tears to my eyes. I didn't want him to see them. That quick glance sideways meant that I caught a sly mocking smile from Frankie at my discomfiture. It was gone in a second, leading me to wonder if I had imagined it. A tearful face was presented to Tenby, and he turned and walked away from us both. Without that glance I would have accepted Frankie's innocence without a thought. Now I listened to, and studied her with an intense scrutiny. Was she hiding something? Was she not the innocent she pretended to be? Or was she something else altogether? There was no time to think any more about Frankie, or even question her further. The police action took over and we were politely asked to leave. Frankie disappeared in her company car with a wave.

***

Jim and I drove off, both of us were silent. I felt I was reaching a breaking point, and I needed a hot shower and a cup of tea. I knew Jim wanted to discuss it further. Not me! I'd had enough of dead bodies, and blackmail. Somehow Jim knew that I had reached a point where discussion was not an option. Several worried glances came towards me from him, as I drove back towards the Priory. But he realised my mood, and sank back into his seat into a brooding silence.

The strange thing was that it wasn't the dead body that haunted my thoughts on that journey back to the Priory. It should have been. Someone's life had been cut short in a brutal fashion, and he had been buried in an unmarked grave. That was horrific, and should have occupied every moment of my thoughts. But no, it was that single place setting in the cottage. The half-drunk mug of tea and the mouldy piece of bread-and-butter sitting on the table. I couldn't get that image out of my mind.

***

After a long hot shower, I had walked the dogs, a short one because I was exhausted. Evening meals were inhaled rather than eaten by my pets and they settled in the lounge, happy and content. It was cool this evening, and my log burner newly lit, was beginning to give out welcome warmth. The pets were tumbled together, asleep on the sofa. I sat in my usual chair and stared at the flames, without even seeing them. The death of Roy Jones had been the beginning of everything. His blackmailing exploits had set off a chain of events culminating in his own murder. The few people I had met since coming to the Priory had been pleasant and seemed law-abiding. Not one of them would I label a murderer. But I had been wrong before. What does a murderer look and act like? Then there was Jim's problem. I knew he was worried, it showed in so many little ways. My fellow residents in the Priory hadn't noticed it. None of them were aware of the surveillance upon him, so didn't realise the intense pressure he was under. But *I* did. I could see the increasing restlessness, the shortness of temper and the deepening of worry lines upon his face. Of course, I noted these things because I knew of the problem. It wasn't because I had deepening feelings for Jim. Oh no. It couldn't possibly be that! I roused myself from my reverie. Time was passing and I had to go to the Priory for my evening meal. All of us not only enjoyed the meals that Maggie and Demelza prepared for us, but appreciated the evening's chat and friendship.

***

The past events were the main topic that evening over a cottage pie with fresh vegetables. My fresh vegetables worked well with a cheese quiche, delicious! Martin got up to make and serve coffee, and make my pot of tea. Maggie was paid to cook for us, and we appreciated her and her delicious food. But not one of us took her for granted, and we all helped out whenever possible.

The loud honking of a car horn as it raced into the courtyard had us all jumping up and rushing to the window. The car drew to a shuddering stop, and a figure got out, gesturing wildly towards us.

CHAPTER TWENTY-THREE

In seconds we were gathered round the car. "It's Demelza," Mary said. "She needs to go to the hospital. That bastard broke into her cottage and did this. Please someone tell her she must go to the hospital. She's refusing to go." Mary's voice ended on a sob, and she opened the passenger door wider.

Demelza looked up at us. She was clutching her arm. Her face was bloodied, and one eye was closed, the bruise on it already forming. Loud swearing from behind me came with a muttered violence deep within it. Sam, who had joined us for dinner was behind me. His swearing continued under his breath. Jim beside us nodded agreement and whispered to him. "We've got to stop this. I have an idea."

"It's no good calling the police. He always has his friends swear that he is in the pub. They always give him an alibi," wailed Mary.

"Two can play at that game," murmured Jim. "Are you up for it Daisy? Sam?" As we both whispered agreement, Jim stepped forward to take charge, as usual.

"Demelza, you must go to the hospital. No arguments. Maggie and Mary will take you to A&E. Maggie can alert Tenby on the way. Photos of your injuries must be taken and logged, no matter if he says he has an alibi or not. No excuses Demelza, that arm is broken."

As Demelza slowly nodded her head in agreement, I drew closer to her. "Demelza," I said to her. She only stared at me with a dejected, defeated look in her eye. "Demelza, we are family. You told me that first time you saw me, and you were right. Families stick together, you told me that as well. Well, this family member is going to solve your problem once and for all!" Demelza stared up at me. I could see that my words had reached through the apathetic fog that her beating had caused. "We'll sort Jason out," I repeated.

"You have my word on that," came Sam's voice from behind me. The emphasis he placed on each and every single word did not bode well for Jason.

Demelza looked from one to the other of us, and I could see her eyes brighten. A small smile crept over her battered face, and she gave a nod at our words which had begun to lift that dreadful apathy that had clung to her.

The beige car drove out of the courtyard. "And how exactly are you going to sort Jason out?" Sheila asked as we stood in the greying darkness of the chilly night.

Jim and Sam watched the car with hard set faces. "We gave our word. We'll sort Jason out." Sam said. Jim nodded in agreement.

"Demelza is my family now. We have to stop those attacks. I don't know how we'll do it, but I want to be there to help!" I said.

"I have an idea," said Jim. "Now! I think that we should act right now. He will never expect that!" Jim said as we trooped back into the kitchen. "Sheila, please call up that pub Jason usually haunts and ask if he's there." While Sheila phoned, Jim stood still. It was obvious that his brain was whirling with ideas, and we all watched him.

Sam's impatience could be seen in the way which he clenched and unclenched his hands. Almost as if he wished he had Jason's neck between his fingers. "I want to beat the living daylights out of him." The words burst from Sam in a cold controlled manner that was truly terrifying.

"You shall have that wish very soon," Jim said softly, his eyes sparkling with the joy of action and intrigue. "Daisy are you up for this?"

"Yes, as Demelza always tells me, I'm family. And I'd like to sort out that bastard. What you want me to do?" I thought longingly of the stash of weapons in my window seat locker. "Do I need…"

Jim interrupted with an appalled look at me, as if he'd read my mind. "No, you, Gerald and I will go with Sam, to the Red Lion pub. It's Sam's birthday and we're going to celebrate it. Sheila and Martin could you go to Jason's pub, and let us know what he is up to?"

"After seeing the state Demelza was in, of course I'm willing to come. Anything to stop him," Martin reassured Jim.

"Of course, we'll help. It's great I can be in the action this time," Sheila bounced in her chair, the white curls dancing in excitement.

"Right, let's get ready and go to the pubs," Jim said.

***

On our entrance into the pub, we made a noisy fuss, with lots of laughter. Jim strode up to the bar and with a loud voice he announced to everyone. "It's this chap's birthday. We're going to celebrate. What are you having Sam? Choose anything you want Sam." Backslapping, loud guffaws and the happy birthday scenario was set up. Everyone in the pub knew it was Sam's birthday, and they all took a good look at him. Drinks in hand we followed Jim to a back corner table, near to the toilets and a back exit to the car park.

Jim's phone rang, "it's Sheila, I'll put her on speaker."

"We've arrived. That guy is bragging about how he taught Demelza a lesson and that they have to alibi him. But two of his friends have refused, and have walked out. But he has two other mates who are willing to lie for him," she said.

"Okay Sheila, sit tight." said Jim and closed his phone. "Right Sam, I'll come with you. When you get Jason out back, then you can threaten him," said Jim.

Sam had been sitting thinking. "No," he looked across the table at Jim. "No, you stay here. I'd rather you coordinated everything, giving me a cover and sorting everything out if it goes wrong."

"But you shouldn't go on your own," protested Jim.

"I'm hoping I won't have to!" Sam grinned at Jim, and then turned to me. "How about it Daisy? You told Demelza that you're family and that you'd fix it."

Both Jim and Gerald protested loudly. "I've got ski masks, black gloves and hoodies with me," said Sam. I had noticed the bag left on the back seat of the SUV; I had wondered what it contained.

"What would Daisy do?" Jim with a worried glance at me, asked Sam.

"Why she will be my backup," said Sam.

Gerald's face was a mirror image of Jim's horrified one.

CHAPTER TWENTY-FOUR

I laughed at their faces. "Sam only wants me as a lookout and a getaway driver, right Sam?" I said and stood up ready for my new role in life, as a getaway driver.

Sam and I drove from the Red Lion to Jason's pub. I parked in a dark corner and turned to look at Sam. "What now?"

"Let's get kitted out whilst we wait," Sam reached over to the back seat for the bag as he spoke. Diving into it he passed me a dark ski mask, dark gloves and a black hoodie. My hoodie was very large, and I had to roll up the sleeves and keep pushing back the hood from my face. "In that pub, the men's toilets are down a dark passage, past a lobby at the back door. It's an exit door from the pub, and also used for deliveries. I shall wait in the lobby and when he goes to the toilet, I'll grab him. Then I'll bring him out to the car park."

I nodded. What could I say? I knew that Sam wasn't going to bring him out for a chat. No way would that work with the bad guy Jason was. I really was ashamed of myself, but I hoped that Sam would teach Jason a lesson. He deserved it, and if it stopped him abusing Demelza, it was all for the good, wasn't it?

"Watch out for me running back to the car Daisy. Then get ready for a fast getaway."

"Okay Sam. Got it!" I grinned at him, feeling foolish as I realised he couldn't see me behind my mask.

"You're enjoying this! You're not a bit scared are you?" Sam's voice was surprised, yet he was laughing at the same time.

"I want that guy to leave Demelza alone, if the law can't do it, we'll have to," was my reply.

"We two could conquer worlds Daisy. You and I

would make an unstoppable team!" Sam said.

The text we were waiting for came in from Sheila. *Jason on way to gents*.

Sam strode off, his steps were quiet despite his bulk. He kept in the shadows. I saw him enter the back exit of the pub, a dark shadow slipping inside. My job had been to stay in the car, and be ready to drive off in a hurry. But I was fidgety. I got out of the car and stood. The door I left ajar. I was only going to walk towards the pub a little way. Just a few steps. I kept looking back at the car. I'd never walked away from a vehicle leaving the keys in the ignition and the door ajar. It went against my careful librarian nature. The shadows along the pub wall were the darkest. The light flickering above the back door, which said exit, only illuminated a small area.

Looking back again at the car, checking it was still there, I crept forward. There was no one around, only a few cars in the car park. The pub regulars were obviously late arrivals, all the better for Sam's chat with Jason. There were the usual wheelie bins. But old-fashioned dustbins had been pressed into service for the recycling sort out. The wheelie bins and dustbins were against the wall, out of reach of the lighted area, and beside them were the darker shadows of the car park. Somehow, I found myself in that darkness, waiting. Just waiting. Another glance back reassured me that the car was still safe, no one had entered it. As my eyes grew accustomed to the darkness, I saw beside me one bin piled high with glass bottles and jars. The one next to it contained cans of every description. Lids had been placed on top of these like scruffy, squiffy caps.

The back door of the pub flew open and two struggling men stumbled out.

"What the hell? Who are you? What do you want?" A harsh voice shouted as the two men struggled. That must be Jason I thought.

"Someone who is going to give you a taste of the medicine you dish out to Demelza!" Sam's voice held a pent-up anger which made me shudder. The struggling men drew closer to me. I edged back towards the wall in my shadowy hiding place. Why did I stay there? Why didn't I run back to the safe space in the car? Punches were now being exchanged, I winced at the thudding blows.

"Put that knife away man! A brawl is one thing, using a knife becomes a police matter." Sam's voice had grown sharp with a dismayed surprise. The knife shone in sudden flashes as Jason flourished it in Sam's face.

"Not so brave now are you? Demelza got brave once, didn't she? I scarred her good and proper. She'll carry my mark on her face until the day she dies!" Jason's voice had now risen to screaming pitch, and he lunged towards Sam.

There was no need to worry, I assured myself. Sam was army trained, and he could handle himself against a knife wielding assassin. Couldn't he? The wheelie bins were my hiding place, as the fighting men drew ever closer to me. I crouched further down, my dark clothes helping me fade into the shadows. Jason was swearing and threatening Sam, who was still backing away from the man. Sam was coiled like a spring ready to attack, but Jason was losing any semblance of reasonable behaviour. I began to fear for Sam's ability to contain this guy. Sam's previous martial training was obvious in his stance, but Jason was becoming ever wilder in his movements and language. Neither man knew I was there, as I blended into the dark pools behind the wheelie bins. They circled round each other, Jason slashing wildly at Sam. Dodging back towards the dark shadows Sam stumbled into a huge pothole in the poorly maintained car park. It threw him off balance, and I saw Jason ready himself to attack. "I'm going to carve you same as I did Demelza!"

CHAPTER TWENTY-FIVE

Voices came from the back door of the pub, and I heard rather than saw two men stand on its threshold. My attention was wholly given over to the struggle taking place in front of me. Jason was looming over Sam who had lost his balance and was struggling to regain it. I saw the knife flash as Jason raised it high above Sam's head.

***

My thought processes were not coherent in my brain. It only took a second before an idea flashed through my head, and I acted upon it. The lid of the dustbin sat lopsidedly upon a bin of overflowing cans, and was directly in front of me. I jumped up, grasped it in both hands and yelled with all my might. "Take that!" Jason half turned towards me. That was his undoing. Wielding the dustbin as if it had been a giant frisbee, I smacked Jason across his face with a satisfactory thunk. "Gotcha!"

He screamed. You'd think that a big man like that would give a big shout. No, he gave squeaky screams, and dropped the knife. His hands flew up to his face to shield it, as I swung back to clobber him again. This time I got his shoulder.

The knife was scooped up in seconds and flung across the car park by Sam. He grappled with Jason before throwing him onto the floor, giving him a few punches on the way down. "This is just a taster. You touch Demelza ever again and I'll be back, and this time I won't go easy on you. Don't ever touch Demelza again!" Sam stepped back from the fallen Jason who was now whimpering on the ground.

"In the car!" Sam hissed at me.

***

I ran to the SUV and was in the driver's seat, the engine running in seconds. I became conscious that my phone had been vibrating with a text. *Two mates looking for Jason.* The text was a bit late. I saw the two men run across the carpark towards Jason. Sam jumped into the car. Before he got the door closed, I was driving out of the car park.

A few moments later, ski masks, gloves and black hoodies were stowed away in the bag on the back seat. We had arrived at the Red Lion car park after my mad dash through the country lanes. I began to shake. Sam was breathing heavily, but it was interspersed with muttered curses. He put his arm around my shoulder. "Calm down, Daisy. You were great, you saved my bacon with that dustbin lid." Then he began to laugh.

"I didn't even think about it, I just did it! That knife of his, and he was so unpredictable, I thought it might give you a chance." My words were coming out, hardly making sense. Sam understood though, and laughed again.

"Always doing the unexpected Daisy, and with the most bizarre objects. Who would have thought you could break someone's nose with a dustbin lid? That guy was seriously crazy with that knife. When I fell into that damn pothole I thought I'd really get sliced up by him. He wanted to do it! And he would have. Daisy you really did save me."

"I broke his nose? I couldn't have, could I?"

My horrified expression made Sam laugh again and he gave me a gentle shove. "Come on Daisy. Let's get a drink inside us both. Remember, I'm celebrating my birthday!"

We slipped inside the Red Lion pub through the back entrance and came in to join the others. They were sitting at the same table, with anxious expressions that cleared the moment they saw us. But I made my way to the bar, waving at them as I went past. "Have you anything else non-alcoholic? I've been sipping my mineral water all evening, and I'd love a change." As the barmaid and I discussed the various non-alcoholic drinks they had, Sam took his place at the table.

"I see the birthday boy is back." She nodded towards Sam. "How is he now? Still sick?" That had been the excuse for Sam's absence.

"No, he's fine now. He's been walking round the car park in the fresh air. Someone mixed up some champagne cocktails for lunchtime celebrations. He's a beer and whisky guy usually."

We laughed together, and she related her previous birthday party mishaps whilst I smiled away. The landlord came out beside her. "Take a break for ten minutes."

She turned away and then looked at me. "I'm making a mug of tea. Would you like one?"

"Would I? You don't know how much I really need that cup of tea!"

Moments later I returned to my seat at the table with a mug of hot steaming tea. Sam had wiped the blood from his lip, but his eye was beginning to discolour, and his knuckles had nasty grazes. I took this in as I sat down, then I looked round at them all. They were all grinning at me.

"Daisy, that was a masterstroke," laughed Jim. "Sam told us about the dustbin lid!"

"My bad, I never reckoned he would be so wild and

crazy with that knife. Thanks Daisy, I reckon you saved me." Sam raised his glass to me and grinned. "Thank goodness, we are on the same side now!"

CHAPTER TWENTY-SIX

Surprisingly enough I slept well that night. As I got into bed, I was certain that I would have dreams of men wielding knives, and dustbin lid frisbees. But my sleep was dreamless. Next morning I fed the animals, got my own breakfast, and contemplated the difficult choice between housework and my beloved botanical painting. It was no contest. Deeply engrossed in a painting of a pomegranate, one full and complete, and one half cut open, I jumped when my phone rang.

"Daisy, it's Martin here. Sheila and I have found another of the men in that photo. We traced him through parish records. He lives in Bodmin with his younger sister. I'll send you the information."

"Thanks Martin, I'll ring my sister, it's really up to her what we do next. As you know, I'm not too sure about all this investigation into our father's background." I washed out my brush, looked regretfully at my pomegranates, and reached for my phone.

It was only half an hour later when we set off on the road to Bodmin. Violet was determined to go to the road, and look at the outside of his house. She drove her car, my Burt's Beefy Bangers van was too conspicuous, and could be easily remembered Violet said with distaste.

"Why do you want to look at the outside of the house? What good will that do us?" I grumbled. I had clutched my seat as she drove away from the Priory, down the narrow winding lanes. Now, as I looked down at my hands, I could see that my knuckles were white, and I was conscious of gritting my teeth. Violet was not a good driver, and she meandered through the town with a careless attitude that made me fear for my life, and those of the pedestrians she seemed to narrowly miss.

"That's the road," I said looking at the notes Martin had emailed to me. We drew up on the road, a few doors away from the semidetached house. It was neat, freshly painted, and the garden well cared for, and beginning to show green spikes from bulbs. As we sat there, a text came through from Martin. *I've just looked on Facebook, found his daughter, who says that he goes to a social centre today. And he is in his 90s.* Martin added the address and we proceeded there immediately.

***

Violet was excited and her driving suffered from it. She drove wildly back through the centre of Bodmin, barely stopping at the crossings or lights in her eagerness to reach the centre. We drew up outside the building surprisingly in one piece. I unclenched my hands from the seat, and shakily undid my seatbelt, patting it with grateful thanks. Both of us got out and stood looking up at the building. It was a large house built around Victorian times, I guessed. Large windows at the front were from floor-to-ceiling. Lights were on inside, because it was a grey gloomy day. There was activity going on, people moving about in the room to the right of the front door, those on the other side of the door were seated around tables.

We walked up towards the noticeboard which proclaimed it to be an activity centre. Some of the days were for children, playgroups and mum and toddler groups. Other days were set aside for the older age group. Wednesdays were for Sunny Seniors, another day was called Fun for Seniors. I grimaced at the labels. I began to wonder if the same activities for Happy Tots Days were the same as those for Sunny Seniors!

"What do we do now?" Violet said as we walked

slowly towards the door.

"We both go in to try and find Humphrey Johnson. I think we'll have to just see what happens."

Today was obviously Senior's day. Each room had a group of older people engrossed in activities. Several helpers were chatting, or just listening to them as they were involved in jigsaw puzzles, card making and board games. We stood in one doorway, where there were two tables with jigsaw puzzles. A young woman came up to us, smiled and made to walk past us.

"Excuse me, our mother is in her nineties, and we wondered if this would be the ideal place for her to visit. She's still very sprightly and alert for her age. Do you have many people of that age here?" I said, seeing Violet's nod of approval out of the corner of my eye.

"Oh yes, one of our regulars. Mr. Johnson is ninety-one, he's at the jigsaw table over there. Do come and meet him." She smiled at both of us, and ushered us across the room.

At the jigsaw table, voices were becoming raised and there was a heated argument developing between two of the group. "Don't put that piece there, that's sky not ocean. The sea pieces are green, you stupid old woman!" A man, a thin droopy figure, sat with his fists clenched in anger as he shouted at the gentle white-haired woman opposite him. "Can't you even do a jigsaw?"

To my utter astonishment she ignored him, and continued placing sea green pieces, complete with waves in the sky part. Then she smiled sweetly at him. "There Humphrey, I've nearly finished it, haven't I?" Was she muddled? Or was she teasing him?

No matter what her intention, enraged at her folly, Humphrey swept the entire puzzle box and board with his thin arm onto the floor. He crossed his arms and glared beneath bushy eyebrows at her.

"Oh dear Humphrey, that won't do at all." The kindly helper began picking up the pieces from the floor and placing them onto the table. "Now then, if you argue like this every time you do the jigsaw puzzles, you won't be allowed to use them."

At her kindly meant remarks, a torrent of abuse came from the elderly man. Cursing, the swear words began to spew from his mouth. Words I'd never heard of, and I was glad that I didn't know what they meant, were shouted at the top of his voice. I walked round the table to peer closely into the man's face. Violet grabbed my sleeve, and gestured with her head to the door. Almost dragging me out of the jigsaw room, she pulled me back to the car. "That's it! You were right Daisy, this is a fruitless task. What a horrid old man, the other one was just grumpy. This man was downright nasty. You don't honestly think he could be our father do you?" The look of horror that flashed across her face made me laugh.

"No, I'm certain he couldn't be our father. He had brown eyes. Our mother has blue eyes, we both have blue eyes, that means our father should have blue eyes as well. I don't think he could be related to us at all."

"You are certain," was her anxious reply.

"I've looked it up and that seems to be the general opinion," I assured her.

"That's great, I'd hate to have him as our father. He was such a nasty old man."

Violet drove home. We drove in silence until I finally spoke. "You have asked her? Why didn't our mother tell you who he was? Did she ever give you a reason? Or even a hint?"

There was silence from Violet for a moment, and then she sighed. "Daisy, you have to remember that it wasn't until I was much older that they told me that she was my mother. For most of my childhood she was my very much elder sister. Then when I realised who she was, I began to ask her questions. But it was useless, she'd either get angry with me, or worst of all she'd begin to cry."

She gave a sudden shriek as we rounded a bend. Face to face with a large delivery van we came to a juddering stop. Violet backed into the passing place, with jolts and swear words. As we continued our journey, I spoke softly to her. "No wonder you let the matter drop. I can understand it now if that was her reaction every time you mentioned it."

"Let's leave looking for our father, shall we? Perhaps we would be better off not knowing," Violet said sadly she drove into the courtyard of the Priory.

"There were three men in that photo, we've done two of them. Let's do the last one and then we forget all about it," I suggested, stooping down to speak to her before I closed the car door.

"Yes, that would be okay. One last go, and then we forget it." She echoed my words, and then reversed the car out of the archway, grazing her paintwork only slightly on the stone walls.

CHAPTER TWENTY-SEVEN

"What the hell were you all thinking of?" Demelza burst into the kitchen and began shouting at us. It was morning coffee time. Her black eye was now purple, and the bruise down her cheek was a yellowing greenish colour. Her arm still in plaster, lay in its sling.

Jim was getting more anxious about the surveillance upon him, and consequently was becoming more irritable. The unknown Watcher was really beginning to freak him out. My surreptitious glance at him that morning showed that the strain was becoming evident in the lines upon his face.

"If you looked in the mirror this morning, you would see what we were thinking about! The police are powerless with his so-called alibi's every time he beats you up. So we took action!" Jim shouted back at her. Silence greeted this outburst and Jim looked chastened. "Sorry," he muttered shamefacedly.

Entering the kitchen for his morning coffee, Sam gave an almighty snort and guffaw. He had been painting in the apartment where he was continuing with the renovations. "It was Daisy, she was the one who took action! If you must blame anyone, blame her!" With an unnecessarily gleeful grin he pointed straight at me.

"Family Demelza. That's what you always tell me. We do anything for our family," I said lamely, and then I began to wilt under her basilisk stare.

"You were there Daisy? You didn't go with them, did you?" She shot a horrified look at me. "Don't tell me that you joined them?"

"Joined them? Daisy was the one who saved the day. Shrieking like a banshee she was when she attacked Jason, and broke his nose!" Sam added.

"Not Jason? He's tough and really mean with it," gasped Demelza.

I couldn't help laughing at her expression. It was priceless. The normally unflappable Demelza was really horrified at the thought that I had gone and helped beat up her ex-husband.

"Family Demelza! You are always telling me that we always help out family," I repeated.

"She's kidding me. Daisy didn't go with you, did she? She could have been hurt." Demelza looked around bewildered.

"Was Daisy there? Not only was Daisy there she saved me from the brute. He nearly had me in difficulties, but it was Daisy who saved the day," Sam said.

Sam gave me an appreciative look. "Daisy always does the unexpected with the most bizarre weapons. She sloshed him across the face with a dustbin lid, and broke his nose. You should have heard him squeal!"

Demelza's one good hand was flung over her mouth, and she sank down on a chair. "Daisy, I can't believe it, you actually broke his nose."

"I kept thinking of your broken arm and I got really mad. I was crouched down behind some wheelie bins, and the dustbin of empty bottles was beside me. The lid was just lying on top of the bottles. When I saw he was flashing a knife at Sam, and Sam had lost his balance, I just acted. In seconds the lid was in my hands, and I did a Frisbee type throw at him. It stopped him."

At my remarks, Sam put his head in his hands, and laughed and laughed. "Yes Demelza. It stopped him, just as Daisy said."

"Does he know who attacked him?" Martin asked with a worried frown.

"No," Demelza shook her head. "His mates have turned on him. When he returned to the pub, he told them that it was in retaliation for breaking my arm and beating me up. At that they got up and walked out. Said he deserved it, and everything he got. But no, not one of them knew who had done it."

"Thank goodness," a relieved Martin sank back onto his chair.

"They were talking about it in the shop this morning," said Maggie, who had done an early-morning shop. "His mates said that he'd gone too far this time, and if he touched you again, they'd beat him up as well."

"Thank you but, Daisy he could really have hurt you…" Demelza muttered, and she gazed at me in dismay.

"Not Daisy! She's a lethal weapon all by herself! She uses whatever is lying around her," Sam said.

"Great. Now then, let's get on with your friend Mary's problem," Jim interrupted, weary of the subject.

"We've come to a stop, haven't we? We're really stumped this time," sighed Sheila.

"No, I've been busy. Daisy had a great idea. When I was in the community shop and post office, I said we'd take any boxes of dead fish or letters to the police. They could leave them here anonymously, without the blackmail threat." Maggie said this with great pride and grinned at me. "I'm sure we'll get a lot of people bringing them," Maggie added

"But I didn't suggest that you go around canvassing the idea, I just meant that if we thought anyone had one," my voice tailed away. I was horrified at Maggie broadcasting my chance remark in such a manner.

"I think it could work, it would get us some info, even if it was anonymous," said Sheila.

"I don't know," mused Jim. "I suppose it may well bring in a few boxes. But without the blackmail threat and the drop-off point I don't know that it will be of much use to the police. Possibly you were right Daisy, after all, we don't care why they're being blackmailed, we are just looking for clues to the blackmailers identity. A second blackmailer and a murderer, we must find out his identity before he kills again!"

CHAPTER TWENTY-EIGHT

The post van trundled into the courtyard. It stopped in the middle, and an elderly man climbed out of the driver's side, and went to the back door. Moments later he was struggling towards the Priory kitchen door with an armful of parcels and letters. Martin and Maggie went out to help him. He followed them into the kitchen, looking very much at home.

"Harry always used to do this round, and it always seemed to happen at coffee time!" Maggie said smiling at the older man, who took a seat at the table as if he'd never been away.

"Don't know how that Roy managed to get the best round. He seemed to push me out of it, but it didn't do him any good in the long run. Same with that other chap who followed Roy. Got my rightful round back now." Harry said as he took a large slurp from his coffee mug. A chocolate chip cookie was dipped into it, and eaten with relish.

"Harry," Maggie walked towards the counter with Tenby's post which she left in a pile for him. We each had our mail in separate piles in front of us, all left unopened, as we watched Maggie. It was obvious that she was up to something. "Harry, you heard about the blackmail that Roy was..."

"Disgraceful! That's what it was. Couldn't imagine Roy being like that. Try to think the best of everyone I do. Then I discovered he was a blackmailer. Disgraceful! Didn't know when he was well off, nice wife and home, he had. Wish I'd a nice wife and home. Didn't deserve it."

"When Roy was murdered, we thought that was the end of the blackmail. But it wasn't!" Maggie declared this with dramatic intensity. She was enjoying herself now.

"It wasn't?" Harry held his second biscuit up halfway to his mouth, he looked horrified at this latest news. The soggy biscuit was now far too sogged. Gravity took over and half of it broke off, landing into his coffee with a plop. Harry didn't even notice. "More blackmail? Oh no!"

"Yes, but this time the letters come with threats," continued Maggie.

"And dead fish, don't forget the dead fish!" Sheila interrupted. She looked positively gleeful at this bizarre twist in the story.

"Dead fish?" Harry looked from one to the other of us, now completely bewildered.

"An old Mafia tradition was to send threats accompanied by a dead fish. This was a sign to show that if they didn't comply, they would join the fish at the bottom of the river, or the sea." Jim explained.

"This is Cornwall, not Italy," said Harry. "Who would think of a wicked Italian custom and do it in Cornwall? Only Italian I know of was Gino, married to your Annie. Died a few years back."

"I know, it's not only weird, but it's crazy. That person stole some of Roy's blackmail letters that he was getting ready to send out. They are now using them to get money themselves. Harry you can help us find out who's doing it, and then we can stop them," said Maggie.

"I can?" The grizzled weather-beaten face scrunched up in puzzlement. "But how can I? I'm not doing anything wrong. I'm not going against the postman's code," Harry said emphatically, looking up at Maggie with misgiving.

"No, no, nothing like that. The threatening blackmail letters come in a parcel. They are the size and shape of a shoebox, or sometimes smaller. But they all have the name and address in green ink printed in large capital letters," said Maggie.

"A stupid dramatic touch," muttered Jim.

"But I…" Harry began speaking.

"All I want you to do Harry, is to look out for them. Tell me who is getting them and leave it all to me," explained Maggie.

"And what…" Harry began again.

"That's all you need to do. Remember Harry you are helping these poor people. That parcel will contain not only a threatening blackmail letter but a dead fish. Think how frightened they'll be when they get it," Maggie continued explaining.

"That's not right. Never in all my days have I heard of such a thing." Harry stood up, both cookies eaten, even the soggy bit at the bottom of his coffee mug. "So this is another blackmailer and this one murdered Roy? And possibly that other postman Luke? I didn't like Luke. He was too nosey, too nosey for his own good."

"Very possibly. Not only is this person a murderer, but is acting in a very peculiar manner with this dead fish business. I don't like the idea of someone like that wandering about the village and living amongst us," said Jim.

"No, he's got to be stopped," agreed Harry.

"Or she, equality remember," muttered Sheila in an aside to me under her breath.

"I'll do it Maggie. After all I'm not tampering with the post am I? You can count on me Maggie." At that definite answer, Harry stomped out the kitchen to his van.

"Well done Maggie, but that took longer and was so much harder than it needed to be," sighed Jim.

"Tell me about it. Harry was always slow and sure in his thought process, but he's getting worse. But if he says that he will do something, you can be certain that he will do it," replied Maggie. "I heard that he has to leave his cottage, he has lived there for over seventeen years. He has been trying to buy it, but can't raise enough money. Such a shame, I can't think why the owner won't let him stay there. Annie says he has gone strange with this cottage business. He was always a great friend of theirs, especially Gino, but he can hardly speak to Annie now."

"Surely we'll get some news about the parcels now. We have the postman and everyone that was in the shop. They will tell their friends and anyone else they can find. Great idea of yours Daisy!" Sheila said thoughtfully, and then she sat up and looked at us. "But we can't just sit here waiting for information. We have to act. And we must act now before there's another death!"

***

The next morning it began. Martin called it the Flipping Fish Fiasco, whilst Sheila said it was the Dead Fish Debacle. Jim just snorted, glared at me and said it was worse than the puppies. "After all they weren't dead, and didn't smell!"

When Maggie opened the Priory front door, which was never used, she found the first one. All of us, and all deliveries came in through the archway into the courtyard to the Priory kitchen door. The small country lane approaching the Priory divided into two, one branch led to the front door, the other to the courtyard. Every morning, Maggie always checked the front door porch in case parcels had been left there. "Someone obviously crept down the lane to the front door. That way they avoided the cameras and lights in the courtyard." Maggie spoke as she carried the box through to the back kitchen. The smell of the fish came in waves behind her as she walked. "Shout out to Tenby, his car is still here."

Whilst Sheila texted Tenby, Jim gestured to me and took his phone out of his pocket. We both rushed after Maggie. I grabbed rubber gloves which were always beside the sink. I put them on and lifted the lid. The smell was appalling. Another sad goldfish lay on its usual bed of kitchen towels, the letter beside it.

"It's not all of the letter. Part of it has been cut off," Jim exclaimed. The camera on his phone clicked endlessly as I held up the part letter. The threat was there in the usual block letters in green ink. Silence would cost this person £250. "They've cut off the pickup place" said Maggie peering over Jim's shoulder.

"Okay what is so important?" The booming voice of Tenby came from the kitchen corridor. We made a great team Jim and I. His phone disappeared into his pocket and the yellow gloves were back beside the sink in seconds. "What the hell?" He strode towards counter and the fishy box. Our explanation was met with grunts, and those beetling brows of his drew together as he gave us his steely glare. "Opened it? More fingerprints on it I suppose."

"No, I used gloves," and I pointed to the sink.

"I didn't realise what it was, so I carried it in. It was Jim and Daisy saw the green writing," Maggie said.

"Why was it left here?" Tenby demanded. All heads and all eyes swivelled towards me. "Daisy! I might have guessed. Okay, I'll take it to the station."

I had to explain, it was obvious, but I really hoped Tenby would take it the right way. "I knew so many people would be frightened to bring the boxes to you, in case their secrets leaked out. I thought if they gave most of what arrived, without the secret, that might be better than nothing at all."

He grunted, again I got that steely glare, but this time

it was accompanied by a nod of the head. Walking to the door he paused and looked back at all of us. "I heard there was a bit of bother in a pub last night. I heard that Demelza's ex-husband got beaten up." There was a silence, and he looked again from one of us to the other. He smiled at us, and then continued talking. "I heard that his nose was broken by fat little person wielding a dustbin lid." He went out of the door and walked down the corridor.

"I am not a fat little person!" I protested loudly.

His chuckles could be heard all down the stone corridor as he walked out of the back door.

CHAPTER TWENTY-NINE

That was the beginning. Two more parcels arrived, all the letters had the secret and the drop off details removed.

"Still goldfish," muttered Jim. "That's four goldfish. How many letters were taken from Roy's shed. Daisy have you any idea how many steamed letters could have been taken?"

"No, I think it was quite a few. That line that he had clipped them on to dry was empty. It could have held about eight or nine I think," I replied.

"Still goldfish," he said and looked at me.

"I don't want to go back to that house or that garden." The horrid house by the river had the biggest goldfish pond in the area. The house was empty, the ideal spot for our blackmailer to find the fish. When we had looked over the house I had been disturbed and upset by what we had found in the kitchen. It still haunted me. The half-finished solitary meal in the kitchen had been upsetting. It had been clear that the diner had obviously died in the middle of his meal, or had been taken ill and rushed to the hospital. Then the body slid from beneath me to erupt into the hole beside Frankie. I still had nightmares about finding Luke's body. That had been the final straw.

"I know you don't like the idea of going back, but I think we should sort out a time to go back there and have another look round the pond," said Jim.

Sheila couldn't come with us, she was having a bad flareup of her arthritis, and found it difficult to walk around. That narrow path and climb down towards the river would be too much for her. As for Maggie, both Jim and I were uneasy at bringing her into our semi-illegal activities during an investigation. Maggie and Tenby were conducting a secret romance. They thought it was a secret, but everyone knew about it. Taking Maggie along on our trips could place her in a difficult position with Tenby. So was it only going to be Jim and myself? Not necessarily something to look forward to.

***

I retreated to my study. An upstairs bedroom now held my botanical painting clobber. Whenever I could I went up there to paint. My latest paintings were of vegetables. I had a large cauliflower on my table. It was the third one. My previous ones had yellowed, and the white had become black in places. But I had photographed it from all angles. The initial drawing I had made was at hand, measured out and drawn in detail. This third cauliflower I used for its colours, the reality of it in front of me, kept a freshness and naturalness in my choice of colours. The final brushstrokes on the painting I found exhausting. Tension crept over me. So many hours of work could be destroyed, and the painting rendered useless by any mishap. A large splash of water, paint colour that didn't quite match, or that final last brushstroke in the wrong place. There were no way mistakes could be rubbed out in watercolour!

It was finished. I stood up and walked around the room. Stretching my muscles, especially those tight tense shoulder muscles, I paused and looked down at my painting. Don't touch it anymore! In my head I heard those words from my last art tutor. My biggest failure in painting was an urgent need when my painting was finished, to fiddle with it. Inevitably I ruined it. It was now dry, so I placed the protective cover over my painting. The cauliflower I put to one side, Maggie had had the last two, and made use of them in the kitchen. I cleared my desk, putting the finished painting on one side. Now came the exciting part in painting. What was I going to paint next? Fresh asparagus was coming into season in a local greenhouse. Maggie had got some from the guy who grew it this morning. There would be a lot of green of course, but the exciting pinks and faint purple colours were evident in the stalks. Yes, quite possibly I'd paint a bunch of asparagus next.

Flora, Lottie and Cleo each had a basket in my study. They often joined me, acting as alarm clocks if I got lost in a painting. Approaching mealtimes would be indicated by a licking of face and paws by Cleo. Scratching and scrabbling in her basket would be Flora, her blanket being moved about, and then finally flung out onto the floor when she became overcome by the pangs of approaching desperate hunger. But it was Lottie who always alerted me and forced me to put down my paintbrush. What did she do? Nothing. She just sat there alert and still, but with an intense fixed stare at my back. How did she do it? That penetrating stare seemed to bore a hole between my shoulder blades. "Okay, we'll go downstairs. And of course I'll feed you. Come on guys, let's go."

***

Fed and watered, and now pottering in the garden as I cleaned their bowls, I watched them from my kitchen window. Three pets, all individual characters, all had bonded together in a tight little group, yet remained such different individuals. My phone vibrated; it was a text from Jim. *Now! My place!* Immediately I called in my pets. They were delighted to come in, and have an unexpected treat. They rushed in to see who could be nearest to the log burner. It was springlike during the day now, but the nights still held a chill. After they were settled, I flung on my jacket and rushed next door. Jim was not an alarmist, and he was always polite, even in a text. That text had been far too brief to be normal for Jim. I knew the constant surveillance upon him by persons unknown had freaked him out. What now? My thoughts were in a fevered worry over what I would find when I pushed open his front door. It was ajar, but I very cautiously looked round the door before stepping inside.

***

I opened my mouth to speak, but Jim was beside me in a moment, his hand over my mouth, and his arm shoving me to one side of the door. Then he pointed. It sat on the table. In the middle of the table was a large stone with a black sign painted on it. Jim gestured for me to move outside. I edged my way back around the front door and outside into the courtyard. Still, he held his hand over my mouth, slowly removing it. With the other hand he placed a finger on my lips. Understanding, I nodded. Then he gestured for us both to walk out of reach of those watching cameras over his front door, the ones installed by the Watcher, the others by Jim himself. The words tumbled out of Jim in a huge rush. So unlike the calm manner which he usually talked. "It was sitting there when I got in. I'd been for a walk. My locks and alarms are useless against this guy. He's really good!" A hand was thrust through his silver hair. "What the hell Daisy? Who's doing this to me? And why? What do they want? Perhaps they want nothing. Perhaps they just intend to drive me crazy." He started pacing up and down the courtyard.

As he reached me at the end of his pacing, I put a finger on his lips this time. "Jim! Jim, just shut up!" That got his attention. His eyes widened and his jaw dropped.

"Shut up Jim. You are now babbling. Come on back to my cottage."

His face changed in an instant. That worried expression was replaced by a growing smile. Then it became more. An expression on his face that I had never seen before, took my breath away. He stepped closer to me and put his hands on my shoulders. "Daisy, oh Daisy." Jim said the words in a deep broken voice.

Lottie, Flora and Cleo had taken possession of the window seat. Action such as this was most unusual in the courtyard. Their worried barking caused us both to turn around. "Come on into my cottage. The pets are barking, they'll set Maisie off, and the others will come to see what's going on." I said, eager to get away from the strained atmosphere that had arisen between us at those words from Jim. I went to the cupboard and poured out a glass of whisky. I practically pushed him into a chair, put the glass in his hand and told him to drink it. "Do you think you should contact Tenby? You've kept this between myself, and Sam. Wouldn't it help if you told the others, especially Tenby? Drink that and calm down, I'm going to put the kettle on for myself." I went into the kitchen area, put the kettle on, placed a teabag in my mug, and stared out of the window. I was at a loss. Jim, the capable man he was, was not used to his life being out of control. This constant surveillance, the unexplained activity in and out of his cottage was causing Jim so much mental anguish I was beginning to worry about his health. If he told Tenby about it, that would help, wouldn't it? I made my tea, admitting to myself that I was taking my time over it. What was I going to say to him now? How could I calm him down? Grabbing my mug, I took a deep breath and turned back to the lounge.

"I can't work it out. How the hell is he getting in? And…what the hell does that stone mean?" His words were getting jumbled, and Jim seemed unable to formulate them in a coherent sentence. Any one of us would feel violated at the entry of a burglar, but for Jim whose very existence and life had always depended on the security of his home, it was a hundred times worse. "Why leave a stone on my table? What does the sign mean?"

CHAPTER THIRTY

Lottie and Flora erupted into barks of excitement, Flora whirling around the room. It was Harry the postman. To my pets relief and joy he had reverted to the old way of posting our mail through each individual cottage letterbox. Lottie grabbed the letters dashing around the kitchen and lounge. Thankfully they were always left intact, and when the dance was complete she handed them to me with only a slight soggy end. Harry went back to his van and rummaged around inside it. Emerging from the back of his van he came towards me with a couple of boxes in his arms. "Here you are. Two of my ladies gave them to me for you. They have no idea why they received them. Neither of them has got any dark secrets. Neither of them wants the police to be involved, and asked if you could deal with them quietly."

Maggie had wandered out of the Priory kitchen down to Harry's van. She often came out for a chat and to take the bulk of the Priory post in with her. Jim had heard the barking and the van stop in the courtyard, and he had also joined us.

I looked at Maggie. "If you'd rather stay out of our investigations, I do understand."

"Why would I stay out of them? Why would I want to?"

Speechless, I could only flounder about trying to think of something diplomatic to say.

Jim gazed at me, shook his head and turned to Maggie. "We know you and Tenby are friendly, and we don't want our activities to jeopardise your relationship," said Jim.

"What I decide to do to help my friends is my decision. No one can change that!" Placing her hands on her hips she glared at us. "I am one of this gang, and I don't want to be left out. If I need to, I will lie to Tenby. And if he doesn't like it, he knows what he can do!" Hands on hips, her black curls bobbed with a vigorous emphatic assurance to us that Maggie was in charge of her own destiny, and her own decisions. I'd seen Tenby watch her with a look of devotion in his eyes. There was no way he'd jeopardise their relationship. Plausible deniability was his only way out of this situation with Maggie. Trust between them would be absolute, but not when it came to our more devious illegal activities. It was always Jim who picked the locks, organized the midnight expeditions, and stake outs. Maggie could always blame him. Harry had reached us carrying the two parcels. But the aroma reached us before he and the parcels did.

"The Priory back kitchen!" I exclaimed. That smell and those parcels were not coming into my kitchen, and I hastily closed my cottage door behind me. Harry held out the stinky parcels. Maggie and I stepped back behind Jim. With a grunt of distaste, he took the parcels and strode towards the Priory kitchen door. We all trooped after him, even Harry who looked hopefully at Maggie.

"I was just about to put the kettle on," she said to him, laughing at his smile of delight.

He sat down in the kitchen, and waited patiently for his mug of coffee and piece of cake. Martin arrived, and he and I followed Jim who plonked the two parcels down on the scrubbed pine table in the back kitchen. Both parcels had notes attached, and they were addressed to me. "Hi Daisy, we have smiled at each other in the shop. I don't know what this is about. I have no secrets to hide. I don't want to go to the police, but heard you and your friends were investigating." I passed the letter to Jim and opened the box. Lifting the lid off carefully and slowly, I reared back in horror as the smell hit me with its putrid force. Another poor goldfish lay on its paper towel bed. Green letters in block capitals again spelt out the words. 'I know your secret. Put £250 behind the litter bin in the shop car park at four o clock.' Martin and then Maggie came to peer over our shoulders at the letter and goldfish. Gritting my teeth, I moved from the first fishy box and onto the second one. Another sad little fish stared glassy eyed up at me. The letter was creased this time. Obviously crumpled up in anger, it had then been smoothed out. Much like the first, the blackmail attempt was couched in the same vague terms. 'I know your secret. If you don't want the entire village to know pay me £300.' It was the same pickup point, but fifteen minutes later.

"Come on, let's go and have our coffee. And I have freshly made chocolate cake!" We left the sad fish in their boxes, and followed Maggie into the kitchen.

***

"It's very good. I reckon that's the best chocolate cake you've ever made!" Harry said, crumbs flying from his mouth as he did so. "Have you heard about old Arthur? Having that Roy use his shed for the blackmail letters has decided him. Daughter has been after him to sell the house for years. She had even got an agent round to give him a valuation." Harry paused to take yet another bite of coffee cake, his second piece, and enjoy its flavour before continuing. He seemed oblivious to our impatience. "Yes, well. He was out shopping. His daughter gave that the estate agent girl the keys to look round and value it. Didn't know a thing about it did old Arthur, not a clue. It's valued now, and apart from a tidy up, its ready to sell. Alright for some, wish I had a house to sell, and a daughter to look after me. Owner wants me out of my

145

cottage, been there for seventeen years. Now he wants to sell it, but won't suggest a reasonable price so I can buy it. Be out on the streets I will, out on the streets! Got to get the necessary to buy my cottage. That's what I'll do. Get the necessary." Harry reluctantly rose to his feet, obviously anxious now to make up the lost time on his round.

"Interesting. So the daughter and the estate agent woman must have seen inside that shed. They may have only looked through the windows. But both of them must have wondered what Roy had been doing. So if one of them has been inside the shed and seen and understood...." Jim's voice faded away as he thought about this new information.

"Poor Harry, he's made that cottage into a little palace, and the garden is an absolute dream. I can't imagine what he will do if he has to leave it. I'm free this afternoon," said Maggie. "What investigating have you lot planned? I want to do my bit catching this guy."

All eyes swiveled towards Jim. "I'd like to visit that house by the river, and check out the goldfish pond again. So many poor goldfish are being killed, the blackmailer may be getting careless."

"But I can't come," said Martin. "I have that computer guy coming round, I shall have to miss this investigation" he told us, but I thought he was delighted having a legitimate excuse for not joining us.

"Daisy and I are going for a second look; we may consider buying it. We are having you with us for your opinions on the property. That will be our story. Are you coming Maggie?"

"No way! I will never set foot in that house again," I exclaimed.

"We are going to check it out Daisy, not buy the flipping place!" Jim snapped at me.

Silence fell in the kitchen. Everyone looked at Jim. "Sorry, Daisy I'm sorry." He raised his hands in surrender at his remark. Jim never lost control in any way. Least of all in his speech. That snappy remark to me was so unusual. I was worried now. Jim was nearing breaking point.

***

Maggie drove to the house. Jim sat beside her, subdued for him. He had been appalled at his outburst, so uncharacteristic of him. I sat behind them, hoping I wouldn't freak out when I went down that garden.

"Here we are. Oh Daisy, you're right. This house looks really creepy and horrid. Let's get it over with," Maggie said when she drew up outside the house.

"At least it's daytime, everything looks worse at night," I said.

Overgrown branches and brambles grabbed our ankles and whipped our faces when we walked along beside the house. Unkempt, this path still bore the imprint of occasional use. Looming above us, the dark shadow of the building cast a coldness and a presentiment of evil as we followed Jim down to the river. "They were hoping to have a dock for kayaks and canoes. All these uneven holes and diggings were for the foundation posts," I explained to Maggie. "That's where we found Luke." Silence fell between us, our footsteps the only sound as we walked past the taped area.

"That river is no more than a stream in the summer, in winter it can be a raging torrent along here. I don't think it suitable for canoes or kayaks," scoffed Maggie.

Nearer to the stream, I could now see what she meant. It was winding amongst rocks and gravel, and was not very deep. Another spell of dry weather and it could dry up completely. A bit further on we came to the goldfish pond. It was deep at one end, but shelved into a muddy patch at the other end.

"There are footprints here," exclaimed Jim as he stood beside the mud. "But it's no good, they are in a complete muddle. It would be difficult to tell which is which, and impossible to find out who they would belong to." The fish in the pond at the sight of him had rushed over, swimming and circling around beneath him.

"They're looking for food. Does the blackmailer feed them? Or does someone else feed them?" said Maggie.

"It's a local lad feeds them every couple of days. Not satisfactory, but surprisingly enough they seem to be thriving," said Jim.

The three of us stood staring at the goldfish swimming around in circles. I felt a bit guilty, standing there with nothing for them. This shallow edge of the pond was muddy, and although there were footprints, there were none to indicate who had been feeding them. When I moved ready to go back to the SUV, there was a glint flashing near to the water's edge beside Maggie.

"Look Maggie, what's that? There's something that sparkles in the light." I pointed and stepped forward. Maggie looked down to where I was pointing.

We both stepped nearer to the water's edge, and Maggie slipped, her shoe sliding in the mud. Her arms flailed out, and she grabbed my shoulder to gain balance, whilst her feet slid further down the muddy bank. Her sudden movements caught me unawares, and I too lost my balance! "Daisy, I've got it!" Maggie cried in triumph as she slipped down, landing with a slushy thump in the mud.

I did a few weird and wonderful movements, my arms waving about to correct my balance. But it was no good. My feet had lost the battle. That muddy patch was just too wet, and I fell beside Maggie. The mud had been our downfall, but at least it was soft enough to land on.

"What are you two doing?" Jim rushed to our sides. His exasperated voice made us both laugh.

"We thought we would have a paddle beside the goldfish." Maggie's initial chuckle became full-blown giggles. "Look! We're having a paddle with the goldfish, they're all swimming round our feet!" They were. The shallow part of the pond suddenly shelved deeply, and both of us had on trainers that had slipped down into that deeper part. Maggie was correct, the goldfish were swimming around our trainers. I would have enjoyed the sight if I hadn't been conscious that my feet were getting wetter and wetter. One cheeky little goldfish was even nibbling one of my laces. "I got it! Look it's a charm, a gold charm from a bracelet. It's a beautiful little piece, it looks very old and valuable. I think it's a fairy, look it has tiny wings." Held in the palm of Maggie's hand, the gold shone brightly in the sunshine. Maggie was correct, this was something unusual and exquisite, and I could see the tiny wings glint as the sun's rays caught their movement in her palm. "Now, all we need to do is to find someone with an unusual gold charm bracelet. Whoever lost this must be furious, it's unique."

By this time Jim, with careful steps towards us had helped us both to our feet. When Maggie and I stepped onto the grass, our feet squelched, and the bottom of our trousers dripped.

"This is awful, I only hope our trainers survive their bath. But I do think it has been worth it, don't you Jim?" Maggie said as she began shaking one foot after the other. At the expression on Jim's face as he looked down at our soggy trousers and muddy trainers, I don't think he agreed with Maggie. His fastidious nature was appalled at the mess our trainers and trousers were in. "I'm sorry

Daisy, that was my fault. I don't know how I lost my balance, but once I did there was no stopping me sliding into that muddy patch and the pond."

After we stomped about trying to clear the mud and slushy water from our footwear, we struggled up the path to the house. Watching our attempts Jim at last smiled. "Okay you two, you are both in a mess, but maybe it has been worth it. That charm is possibly a significant clue that you found."

"Should we show to Tenby?" I asked.

"I don't know, he warned us to keep out of his investigation," said Jim deliberating over the problem.

"This is no longer a crime scene, so there should be no reason for him to question our actions here. Is there?" I answered him. I realised that my words could not phrase the exact description of where we were, or what we were doing. "After all, you can't take a goldfish fingerprint." Foolishly, I sniggered at that remark I made, even though I knew it wasn't really very funny. It tickled Maggie though, and she began giggling as well. We staggered along, trainers squelching and squeaking, clutching each other, and shaking with mirth.

"You two are both…" Words failed Jim and he stared at us as if we were being ridiculous. Perhaps we were, but the stress and upsets over the last few days had to get some release. That silly joke of mine had done it for both of us.

We walked alongside the house, struggled again through the brambles and overhanging branches and came out in the front garden which overlooked the lane. It was as we neared the front gate we saw it. Jim stopped abruptly, I cannoned into him, and Maggie grabbed my arm in dismay. "No! Oh no. Look at that!"

CHAPTER THIRTY-ONE

"The SUV is covered with green paint!" Maggie cried out.

"They've slashed every single tyre!" Jim shouted as he rushed up to the SUV. "Every single one!"

"That paint is still wet. Could only be minutes ago that it happened, there are paint runnels still dripping down to the ground." I said, as I rushed after the other two out on to the road. The SUV was exactly where we had left it, parked in front of the gate. It was no longer freshly washed and polished. Green paint had been thrown on it, all over the windscreen and splattered on the roof. Every one of the tyres had been slashed.

"The decision has been made for us. We definitely have to phone Tenby now." Jim's voice was flat, full of suppressed rage. "In reporting this to him, we'll have to tell him why we were here." Silence as we all thought this problem through. Tenby could be unpredictable in his reactions to our investigations.

"Don't worry about it. This is exactly like the shed. Our nosing about produced results when we discovered what was in Roy's shed. If we hadn't come here looking for the goldfish pond clues, we would never have found the gold charm," I said, more in hope than in certainty.

Maggie brightened and said thoughtfully, "and if we hadn't come here no one would have known that this was where he got his goldfish. The vandalism on the SUV proves that he has been coming here."

"I wonder," said Jim thoughtfully.

"You wonder what?" I asked him.

"Where will our blackmailer get his fish from now?" Jim replied.

"He? Do you still think that it is he? This gold charm

points to a woman. Poison is often said to be a woman's choice of murder weapon." Maggie's words died away as two police cars came barreling down the lane towards us.

The men got out and walked towards us. They stared open mouthed at the state of the SUV. Only one of them spoke. It was Tenby, and he swore. He swore at length. "Fond of green, isn't he? Why were you targeted here? In fact, what are you all doing here? Why now?" Tenby drew those beetling brows of his together in a frown, which he directed at me. "Daisy, what have you been up to now? Not another body I hope?" His sharp eyes took in the state of my trousers and trainers, then he noticed Maggie's were the same.

Maggie opened her mouth to reply to this remark. I put a hand on her arm to quieten her. They were in a relationship. I was uncertain as to what kind of relationship it was. I felt that Maggie should keep out of it, there was no need for their relationship to founder over his remarks to me. I wasn't scared or intimidated by his bad cop attitude. I had seen him crawling around the floor with my fluff ball Flora! I stepped forward. "Not guilty! It was Jim's idea to come and check out the goldfish pond. They are not very good witnesses, no fingers for prints! But it was worth a try. Unfortunately, it was slippery and muddy and Maggie and I joined the goldfish. As we are so wet and dripping, and thoroughly miserable, can we please go home now? Martin has just arrived to give us a lift." I took the gold charm from my pocket. I dropped it carefully in the clean tissue and handed it to Tenby. He was speechless for once, looking at the charm, and our deplorable state. I grabbed Maggie's arm, gave Tenby and Jim a wave, and trotted off to the van. Jim had texted Martin to come in my van and pick us up. He would remain with the SUV, and if needed Martin would return for Jim. My hope of getting into my van for a speedy getaway was halted by Martin who got out of the van, and stared open mouthed at the state of the SUV. "Jim told me about it. This is far worse than I imagined. I thought a small amount of green paint and a couple of slashes at a tyre. This is so very bad."

"Come on Martin, hurry up. My feet are so itchy and soggy," moaned Maggie. "I need a shower desperately and clean dry clothes. This is so uncomfortable!"

We drove away, with a last glance back at the horrific sight of the SUV. "This guy has a nasty vicious streak, he's certainly shown it in this latest attack. How did he know you were there?" Martin said as he drove back down the lanes to the Priory.

"I don't think he did know we were there; I think he was coming to get some more goldfish," I said.

"And we were already there!" Maggie exclaimed.

"He obviously knew the SUV. I wonder if he crept down to look at the pond. We wouldn't have seen him if he'd stayed up beside the house. He'd have seen us messing about around the goldfish pond. He must have been furious to find us there," I said.

"Daisy, you think he was watching us?" Maggie said, obviously unsettled at the very idea.

"If he was, I hope he enjoyed the sight of us floundering about in among the goldfish!" I laughed at the idea.

"You both slid right into the pond? I can see that you are both wet and muddy. What happened?" Martin asked us.

"We thought the goldfish were having so much fun, we decided to join them," snapped Maggie. Her discomfort and annoyance how foolish we both looked overcame her usual good manners. Relenting at this lapse, Maggie told the story to Martin, dwelling on the successful finding of the gold charm.

I looked at Martin, really looked hard at him. He was struggling, it was quite an effort for him. So I took pity on him. "Okay Martin, you can smile. I'll even allow you a little chuckle, but don't you dare laugh at us!"

CHAPTER THIRTY-TWO

Only Cleo found the aroma on my shoes fascinating. Flora and Lottie, both known to have on occasions not only splashed in muddy puddles, and on one memorable occasion rolled in fox poo, sniffed at my trainers in distaste.

Showered, changed and the log burner lit, I put the kettle on for a mug of tea. Whilst that bubbled away I fed my pets. My head was buzzing and full of goldfish, green paint, and wondering about the secrets that drove people to kill. There was a distinct lack of enthusiasm from Cleo after I placed her evening meal down on the floor for her. I looked again at it.

"Oh no! I've given you the dog food!" Grabbing that meal I rushed into the dog's dinner room, actually my front hall. Both dogs were sitting back licking their lips, again and again with obvious enjoyment. They loved cat food. I left them there and went back into the kitchen to open up yet another tin of cat food. A disgruntled Cleo glared at me, walked around her dinner bowl three times, before finally settling down to eat it. Cats!

***

Our meal that night in the Priory kitchen was subdued. Each of us had thoughts to process. The initial excitement of getting the green inked boxes and letters had faded away.

"There's nothing. Not one inkling of a clue," complained Sheila. "Ha! Get it, inkling! All we get is green ink, and now green paint. You'd think he was a leprechaun! There's not been even a decent explosion." Every head swiveled to stare at her. "What? Admit it, this is a nasty spiteful individual, he uses poison, and frightens old ladies and ordinary village people by threatening to expose their secrets. He's nasty and spiteful!"

"Sheila is right. He acts in a sly furtive manner. But why? What is he after? What is he trying to prove?" Martin said.

Sheila sat upright in her chair. Those curls of hers began to bounce again. She clapped her hands. "I've got it! He's probably in the hands of a drug dealer and has to find money quickly. Or perhaps he's fallen foul of a gangland mobster boss. Could it be a gangland war that's broken out?" Silence greeted these remarks. There were shaking heads and a chorus of 'don't think so' — 'unlikely' and other mumbled remarks. Sheila sank down into the chair, her excitement fizzling out. What other octogenarian would be excited and thrilled at the thought of a gang war breaking out on Bodmin Moor?

Maggie put the vegetables on the table. Roast potatoes accompanied by a hot honey roast ham fresh from the oven. The cheesy sauce added the final touch to a delicious meal. I had a quiche with the vegetables, and some of the delicious cheesy sauce. The meal took our attention away from dead goldfish, and all-out gang warfare amongst the pretty Cornish villages.

The motorbike roaring in under the archway alerted us to the fact that Sam had arrived. After securing his bike he wandered into the kitchen.

"Would you like to join us Sam," said Maggie.

"Only if there is some to spare. It looks good, and I'd love a plateful."

The plateful was placed in front of Sam, and he eyed it greedily. After a mouthful, he looked up at us. "Heard you were paddling with the goldfish Daisy and Maggie," Sam said as he piled his plate high again with more roast potatoes.

"Oh no! It's not all round the village already?" Maggie said.

"Yes, and the green attack upon the SUV. It's been added to in the telling. Jim texted me, to warn me to take care of my motorbike. Thanks Jim for that. I often leave it out on the path up to the cottage. It went into the garage after your text, and the door was locked." A large mouthful of ham was chewed, followed by another crisp roast potato. "Yes, the latest story that I heard was that Jim fought with a huge, masked man who wore a green balaclava. Daisy and Maggie were thrown into the goldfish pond by this large intruder, who threw green paint over them."

"But that's ridiculous. Nothing like that ever happened!" Maggie exclaimed, furious at this tale. Sam's grin widened the fury in Maggie's face.

"I don't know, it sounds better than you both just slipped into the goldfish pond," Sheila declared with a laugh.

Jim got a text. "It's from Tenby. Hilda Evans has regained consciousness, but doesn't remember the attack on her."

"Great news," each one of us cried out our delight in different ways. The woman had bought raffle tickets from Jim and I. A few hours later she had been attacked, knocked out and fell into a coma. Now she was conscious, it was a bright spot in our dismal day.

"We've got to get this guy! Two unnecessary murders. Roy and now Luke, both were postmen. Whatever Roy did, and his blackmailing was bad, he didn't deserve to die. And why Luke had to die I can't imagine. Tomorrow morning I'll have an agenda worked out for us. We've got to find this guy, and we will bring him to justice!" Sheila's words rang out around the huge kitchen, echoing even into the shadows. Sheila's remarks were not ideas or wishes for that morning. They were actual promises! Or were they threats?

***

Next morning, I opened the back door to let my pets out for their morning tasks. Lottie was always first out of the open door. That was usually followed by a scamper around outside to sniff out any intruders that may have visited her garden during the night. Not today! Lottie stood stiff on the threshold sniffing the air. A low growling rumble came from deep in her throat. Cleo walked up behind her, ready to go into the garden. Lottie turned towards Cleo and barked in her face, her little nose pushing the cat back into the kitchen. Lottie looked up at me, gave short sharp barks followed by grumbling growls. It was getting obvious to me that Lottie was definitely trying to tell me something. This had to be serious, it was so unusual for Lottie to behave in this manner. I lifted her up, placed her inside the kitchen with Cleo and Flora, and shut the door on them. There had to be a reason why she wouldn't go out into the garden, or allow the other two out.

***

There was a reason! Behind the back gate lay a dead rat, a pigeon and a magpie. Walking gingerly towards the group I saw the cause of their deaths. A scattered group of poisoned titbits had been thrown over the gate. A mixture of raw meat and biscuits lay with the dead animals amongst it. This had been meant for my pets, but the early morning wildlife had feasted on this unexpected bounty. They had died. But their deaths had saved my pets, or rather Lottie had! Tenby rushed round at once after my text. He had been dressed ready for work, and my text had caught him before he had set off for the day. His creative swearing had been enhanced by the other members of the Priory community that had gathered around the poisoned creatures. The forensic guys came again. It had been a depressing thought to realise that we were now all on first name terms. They had begun to greet us as old friends. I even knew how much milk, and how many sugars they liked in their coffee. I didn't tell them, but I hoped that it would be the last time I'd ever see them. It would have been rude considering how pleasant they were. The sad remains and the obviously poisoned stuff was bagged and taken away.

"Surprised it's not green, everything else is usually green," was Jim's sarcastic remark as he joined me. "Vicious and evil, he really has got it in for us now."

I began to shake. Maggie took my arm. "Come on Daisy. You need some tea, and I have some chocolate chip cookies freshly baked."

"It's only eight o'clock in the morning, it's time for breakfast, not for chocolate chip cookies," said Jim, appalled at this departure from normal mealtimes food.

"Daisy needs a strong mug of tea, chocolate chip cookies, and then I'll get breakfast on the go," declared Maggie. Her arm around my shoulder she propelled me towards the Priory kitchen.

"But the guys…" I gestured at my pets, who were trotting around the garden on leads, being kept well away from the danger zone.

"Don't worry about the poison, we'll hose the area down and then we'll place some netting across the back part of the garden. We'll make certain they stay secure and free from any other attacks." Martin for once was decisive and had swung into action. He loved my little guys, and was incandescent with fury at the thought of how nearly they had died.

"Bring them to the kitchen now, they can play with Maisie and have some fun," said Maggie and lifted up Flora.

Lottie was sitting on my foot, as usual. I picked her up and held her out at arm's length. The tiny tail swished to and fro happily, and I'll swear that she grinned at me. "You are the best! Lottie you are the cleverest girl of all. You saved yourself and Cleo and Flora!" I hugged her tight, and she squirmed up to lick my chin.

***

The heat from the Aga was welcoming after we had been standing around in the chilly morning. Demelza rushed up to greet me, as soon as I entered the room. Lottie was delighted at all this hugging, and Demelza got a few licks as well.

"He's gone! Daisy you did it!"

"Who's gone? What did I do?"

CHAPTER THIRTY-THREE

"It's Jason, he's gone to join his brother in Ibiza. He has a bar, and Jason is going to work in it. Daisy, it's all because of you and that dustbin lid!" Demelza grinned round at us all, her smile wide despite her bruised face.

"Why because of me?" I was delighted at the news, but couldn't see how my meagre input could drive a huge brute like Jason abroad.

"He was a laughingstock. When you hit him with the dustbin lid, his mates were at the door, and they heard his squeaky screams when his nose broke. They have told all his other mates."

I remembered. At their arrival at the back door, his two friends had paused for a moment trying to work out what was going on. That had been the signal for Sam and I to race for the car. I was especially fearful of being caught, and being exposed as a geriatric mugger! But I hadn't realised that they had been there in time to see my dustbin trick.

Demelza was still laughing. "They said he was felled to the ground by a little fat person wielding a dustbin lid. His broken nose is just adding to their fun!"

"I'm not a little fat person," I muttered.

"Thanks Daisy, thank you cousin," and I suffered yet another hug. I ignored the other persons in the kitchen behind me. I ignored the hands hiding grins, and the muffled laughter.

Breakfast had finished and Sheila produced her large Agenda book. The conversation came to a halt, and the whole kitchen became enveloped with a solemnity and purpose, unusual amongst us. "It's got to stop! He has to be found, this latest attempt on the pets means that he is unhinged, and is going to stop at nothing to get back at us." Murmurs of agreement greeted her remarks. The attempt to poison my pets had left each one of us appalled at how vindictive the blackmailer was becoming.

"He knows we are investigating, and is trying to stop us," murmured Martin.

"That's because our investigations have had 100% success rate," stated Sheila

"We've only done two," said Jim.

An angry glare was sent in his direction by Sheila. She hated anyone to belittle our investigative prowess.

"Sorry," his hands went up in an apology, and Jim subsided back down in his chair.

"I don't think he would dare go back to that goldfish pond, so where will he get his fish from now?" Maggie asked.

"It's either frozen fish from the village shop or supermarket, or he will get some from the fish van. We need to chat with Eric the fish man, he might be able to tell us more. Or perhaps the blackmailer will look out for another fish pond," Jim said.

We all began to leave the kitchen, with me trying to wrangle my pets, when Annie arrived. A local, born and brought up in the village, she 'did' for everyone. Widowed when young, she had brought up Leah on her own. Annie was indefatigable in her church, village and work-related activities.

"Hello Annie. Watch out, this lot of animals will trip you up if you're not careful. I'm trying to get them back to my cottage, but Maisie wants to come as well."

"It's okay Daisy. I don't mind them. Sweet little darlings," Annie said, and carefully avoided them. A large woman, her short black hair was cut in a mannish style, which gave her stocky build a tough image. She had always been very pleasant to me, but in a stilted aloof way. I sensed that she didn't like animals despite her protestations of affection for them. I also thought that she didn't like me.

This morning I was visiting my mother. Each week I had a special day for my 'alone' visit, and then each Saturday Violet and I went together. Discovering that I had a twin sister and a mother had been traumatic, even if it had been wonderful. My sister and I were feeling our way into a deeper relationship. My mother was erratic in her moods, after all she was in her nineties, and her attitude towards me often varied. So much so, that each visit I approached the care home with nervous anticipation. My life had to be explained and talked through with her every single time. This was absorbed in a quiet solemn manner. If I mentioned my son Jake, her face lit up and she couldn't hear enough about him. Ninety-two years old, but her hearing and intellect had not been diminished by age. Unfortunately her eyesight was poor, but she coped uncomplainingly, loving her audiobooks and had embraced pod casts with enthusiasm. Martin kindly took my two dogs for walks on that morning. I don't know who enjoyed their outing more, Martin or the dogs.

This morning I had determined, if I managed to get up enough courage, that I was going to ask her about my father! Violet had tried and failed many times, perhaps my mother would unburden herself to me. I could only try. It was the first time I had seen my mother not only looking tired, but showing every year of her great age on her wrinkled face. It had been a shock to me. The usual carer who always whispered an update to me as I walked into mother's room was on holiday. The pleasant faced woman who left the room, only smiled as she walked out. No update.

"Daisy I have something for you." The voice was

shaky, but she was as alert as ever. "In that drawer is a box. Papers from my youth, about your birth, are all in that box. I've kept them for you, the eldest should always have the family papers. Violet couldn't cope with it, I know you can cope, you are much stronger."

Retrieving the box from the drawer, I sat with it on my knee. She was tired now. The issue of our father, and the questions I had wanted to ask would have to wait. Perhaps the answers were already there in the box. Maybe I was holding in my hands the very answers Violet and I had been searching for. The tiredness that she was fighting began to overwhelm her, and I rose to leave. Normally she'd ask me to stay longer, but not today. I bent over and kissed the wrinkled cheek. Her hand, a papery skin stretched tightly over it, every vein evident beneath it with the numerous brown age spots gripped my hand tightly. Still surprisingly strong she drew me closer to her. "Daisy, I wish we'd met sooner. I am so pleased to know you and Jake even for such a short time." She drifted off to sleep, her hand dropping from mine onto the bed. My hand felt empty and bereft.

Tears blinded my eyes as I walked out to my van. I placed the box carefully in the back of my van and covered it with an old blanket. I was going for my lunch date with Jeff. This had become a habit. My work would be discussed, paints and paper would be bought, and then we would go for lunch. Jeff and I were mates. We had agreed that neither of us was interested in the other romantically, and now enjoyed the pleasant friendship that had grown up between us. It was strange that we laughed and enjoyed so many of the same things.

***

Whilst driving to Stonebridge, and eating my lunch with Jeff, my mind kept flitting back to the box in the van.

"When are you going to get rid of the van?" Jeff's voice intruded into my thoughts.

"My van? Why should I get rid of the van?" I asked, puzzled by his question.

"I understood you bought it in a hurry when you moved to Cornwall. It was ideal for removing your luggage, and your cat basket at the same time. But now? Surely you want something suitable for your…" His voice tailed away; he was obviously uncertain as how to proceed.

"More suitable for my age and position in society?" I finished for him. My tone of voice and expression must have alerted to him that I was not pleased.

"Well, I was just thinking." Jeff's slightly flushed face betrayed his increasing embarrassment.

"I love my van. The logo BURT'S BEEFY BANGERS is great fun. It's easy to find in a car park, and no one in their right mind would ever consider stealing it. And I can easily transport my painting to your shop, animal cages can be…"

Jeff's hands went up in mock surrender at my increasing wrath. "Okay, okay, you love your van. I get it. It's just that I have a friend who would always get you a good deal on a car."

"If I sell the van, I'd probably get a motorbike," I said thoughtfully. "My pets would love to sit in a sidecar with the breeze blowing."

Jeff had taken a swig of his coffee before my remark, but he spluttered when he realised what I had said, only getting his paper napkin to his mouth in time. "Keep your van Daisy. For goodness sake keep the van. The thought of you on a motor bike!" Jeff visibly shuddered at the thought.

I laughed at him. "You sound like my twin sister Violet. She's always hoping that I will get a more sedate car. She's embarrassed every time that she has to get into my van."

A text came in for me from Maggie, *Demelza has a goldfish parcel.*

CHAPTER THIRTY-FOUR

I drove back to the Priory. Thoughts and concerns about my mother, and the box sitting under its rug in the back of my van, were jumbled in my head with the thought of this latest parcel.

When I got out of my van I heard loud knocking at the window of the kitchen. It was Sheila and her gestures were wild and emphatic. Something is up, I thought as I carefully locked my van. The kitchen seemed crowded when I finally entered. Jim had rushed in from the library and joined the others around the kitchen table. Maggie moved back and made room for me.

"Hi Daisy, come and look at this." She pointed to the parcel, again with capital letters in green ink, with a demand for £500 or else the secret would be exposed. Leave behind the loose stone, it continued just like the other ones.

"Always when it's busy. The last time he paid a kid to get hold of the money. I've got an idea. I think we can get round that and finally grab him," said Jim.

"You have? How?" Martin asked him.

"That shop is on the edge of the open moorland. We all take a spot near the shop and check if anyone sends a kid back for the money, or seems to be suspicious. One of us will wait in the car park, and the others in the approach road to the shop."

"And Tenby? What about him? We are not doing it on our own, are we?" Martin's voice became shrill with apprehension.

"Yes we are!" Jim declared emphatically.

"Daisy, you've got a letter with green capital letters on it." Maggie handed me the letter which was also sitting on the table.

I put some kitchen gloves on first, then opened it with care. There was no fishy smell, and no letter inside it. "Nothing," I said, and held the empty envelope upside down. It wasn't empty. There was a clattering clinking sound on the table and a shiny object slid across it, and spun around before coming to rest.

"A bullet! It's a bullet. The Mafia send the bullet to someone that they have marked out for death!" Sheila shrieked. Was Sheila excited, delighted or appalled at this new development? I couldn't be sure, perhaps it was a mixture of all three emotions.

Without a word, Maggie took out her phone from her pocket and dialed. We all knew who she was calling. Jim took a plastic bag from the kitchen drawer, took my gloves from me and placed the bullet inside it, and sealed it.

"I've been looking up Mafia warnings. This is one of them. Other warnings are when they send the heads of horses, and the latest horrible thing in America is that they send dolphin's heads," said Sheila.

I was angry. Angry at the bizarre manner in which we were being terrorised by the unknown person determined to cause havoc on us and our community. "There's not many dolphins on Bodmin Moor, and they'd need a much bigger envelope." There was silence and everybody stared at me. "Yes, that was an awful remark to make about the poor dolphins. But I'm tired, I'm going to go to my cottage to see my pets." I thanked Martin for walking and feeding them whilst I was out. I wanted to be on my own. A boiling rage had engulfed me. This blackmailer was sneaky and nasty. The constant drip of the blackmailing boxes, and poisonings were getting everybody down. We, as the Priory Five had dealt with evil murderers before. The sheer badness of those guys had been more straightforward. They had been people we had known and what they looked like. The places they lived, and the pubs they frequented had been known to us. The blackmailer was unknown. It could be anyone that we met each day. It could be someone that we trusted and even liked. It was the anonymity that was so disturbing. Somehow this was creepy and sly. I thought of poor Hilda and the cruel attack on her. Roy Evans had been evil in the manner in which he blackmailed, but he hadn't deserved to die. Nor had Luke. I was worried about this second blackmailer's attitude, there was an increasing madness about the number of boxes that were appearing. No longer targeted to the people Roy had singled out with hidden secrets. It was in a bizarre random manner that the boxes were now being posted. Was it a way to make money? If so why do it this way? Where and why this Mafia stuff? Was it from Francesca? She had an Italian uncle. I had the premonition that it was all going to escalate. And I was not ashamed of being frightened.

***

On my entrance to my cottage I was greeted rapturously by Lottie and Flora. As usual Cleo gave me a solemn stare and a sniff, and turned away from me. I should not have gone out, I should have stayed at home and waited on her Majesty. I brought into my cottage the box from my mother. Dark wood, it had an ornate veneered pattern around the top. I placed it on the coffee table, and sat down on the sofa and stared at it. A similar elongated pattern was around each side, in a variety of lighter woods. A key was in the lock. It faced me, dark dull metal with an intricate cutout pattern, and a tiny ribbon hanging from it. It was a faded red ribbon. I sat and looked at it. Lottie licked my hand and gazed up into my face. Cleo had now forgiven me, and was now sitting beside me, her eyes slit in serious contemplation of me. Flora was wriggling around in circles, but occasionally casting an occasional anxious glance in my direction.

The box sat there. The red ribbon hung from the key. "I only need to turn that key. Maybe there is important information inside that box. Even details about my father," I said out loud. Still, I sat there looking at it. "No, not now!" I rose to my feet and picked the box up, ran to my bedroom and thrust it into the top cupboard, as far back as it would possibly go. "Even if it contains the best news in the world, I cannot cope with it. If it's bad news, I'd go to pieces." I explained to my trio of pets, still sitting on the sofa watching me. It was the right decision. Cleo gave me that nod of her head which meant agreement, kneaded her paws on my cushion, then curled up into a ball and went to sleep. Lottie wagged her tail and gave me that special sausage dog grin. Flora snored.

A text came from Jake. *Mum, Lisa's mum needs us to stay longer. Her dad is not doing well. Will phone tomorrow.* No sooner had I put my phone down on the table, then another text came in. *Get ready for the money drop J.* What did one wear to a stakeout and a money drop?

***

The SUV sat at the edge of the common. My van being so conspicuous had been left at the Priory. No one said it, but I knew they meant I was noticeable as well. So I had been placed at the outer limits of the common. Jim had parked in the car park opposite the loose stone drop-off point. But he was in a truck belonging to Sam, and wearing a baseball cap. Strange, it shouldn't have done so, but it actually suited him. Pulled down over his face, he sat in the driver's seat with a newspaper propped up on the steering wheel. Maggie was browsing in the shop. Known to be part of the Priory crowd, she had with great excitement donned a disguise. Large glasses and a scarf wound tightly around her neck, the addition of a beanie hat and a backpack, and she looked a typical hiking tourist. Martin had been placed on the other side of the common in Jim's car. I couldn't work out if he was more nervous of driving Jim's car, or being involved in the stakeout.

I checked my watch. Five minutes to go. Four o'clock had been the time written down on the letter. The blackmailer had been clever. Some schoolchildren were out of school at three thirty, whilst other schools let their kids out at four o' clock. With mums queueing to get into the car park, children and parents milling about the shop, and some standing in groups outside, it was chaotic. That stone could be moved, and it would be impossible to check out who was doing it, and even see them in amongst the crowd. Only Maggie who had been designated the watcher through the shop window, and Jim who had direct observation had any chance of seeing it.

Earlier that morning a package had been placed there, about the similar size that the money would have been. But it contained newspaper and a sticky substance inside it with a dye mixed into the stickiness. Jim's idea to mark our guilty handed! Four o'clock came and we were all ready for the money drop. The eruption of noise from the car park at exactly two minutes before time indicated a problem. Maggie texted me from the shop. *It's chaos here Daisy, some of the kids are arguing and milling around. There's no way I can get a clear view. Check for someone suspicious coming your way and alert Martin.* I relayed the message to Martin, and began to stare intently at every person or car leaving the car park. Then I had an idea. I was still holding my phone in case I got any more text messages. So I held it up, and captured each person and car as they left the car park on my phone. At ten minutes past four Jim drove out of the car park with Maggie seated beside him, and they waved at me to follow them back to the Priory.

***

The baseball cap had been flung on the table, the sunglasses, and Maggie's beanie hat and scarf, and backpack disguise beside them.

"What happened?" Martin rushed in behind me. "Did you see anything?"

"No! Somehow a fight broke out between some kids. That must have been engineered by our so clever blackmailer. Nothing! Useless waste of time!" Jim stomped up and down the kitchen, his frustration obvious to each and every one of us.

"I took video of everyone leaving the car park. Shall we watch it and see if we can spot something or someone?" I said.

Maggie's laptop was placed on the table, and we all gathered round to see the exodus of children and parents from the shop car park.

"Stop it! Stop it right there. I see something," Jim cried out.

CHAPTER THIRTY-FIVE

Jim pointed at the figure hurrying out of the car park. We watched as the figure on the screen jumped into a car parked further along the road towards the common. "Rewind it and slow it down please. We might have something here."

"It's a woman, and she has a suspicious bulge of the right size in her pocket," I pointed as she got into the car.

"Well done Daisy! Take a screenshot of her, and note down all car numbers of those leaving the car park. I doubt we'll get anything from the picture of her even if we blow it up, she's wearing a hoodie, so there's no joy there. But the car numbers might help," Jim exclaimed and pointed again. "There's Francesca getting into a car, I thought it was her. But couldn't be certain being further up the car park."

"That's Harry driving out in his old car. He keeps saying he'll get a new one, but he never does. Funny the postman going to the Post office in the afternoon," laughed Maggie.

The stakeout meeting adjourned, there had been little gained after all our efforts, and we were a disappointed group who went off to do our own thing.

***

Sam joined us for the evening meal. Gerald was visiting a cousin of theirs, one that Sam did not get on with. Sheila was still with the grandkids, helping her daughter out who had embarked upon professional courses. So it was just Martin, Maggie, Jim and I with Sam eating with us.

"I have an interested customer coming to look at a dresser I'm renovating. They are coming tomorrow, and I need to get it finished, so I may well work late. Martin, can I put a camp bed in there with a sleeping bag? You don't mind that do you?"

"I have a spare bed you could always…" Martin began speaking but Sam interrupted him.

"Thanks, but I don't know how late I'll be working. I'd hate to disturb you coming into the cottage. This way when I finish I can just crash out."

"You seem to be selling quite a few items of furniture. Is it going to work out for you?" I asked Sam. It had been at my suggestion that he had gone down the renovating old furniture route. I'd have felt dreadful if it had been a disaster.

That wicked grin of his spread over his face as he looked at me. "Yes Daisy, not only is it working out, it's great! I have some antique dealers and interior design stylists contacting me now. I may need you as a PA to sort out all the paperwork for me. As you said at the time, I'd have no rent, no mortgage and it's absolutely true. The money I get means I can buy superior stuff to do up. That gets a higher price on the resale."

Congratulatory remarks ended the meal, and we all went off to bed delighted at Sam's new venture's success. The day had been one of mixed fortunes for all of us. My thoughts went back to the post office car park fiasco. It had not been a successful stakeout, but had not been a complete disaster. For once I had done the right thing, using my phone had given us some useful information. And I hadn't fallen over, or tripped up. In fact I had achieved my success without any major mishaps for once! A day that had gone reasonably well.

Flora alerted my other pets and myself. That low rumbling growl from her had Lottie giving tiny anxious yips. I sat up in my bed. "What is it Flora? What can you hear?" A quick glance at the clock showed it to be after two in the morning. Cleo was sitting erect, ears pricked forward and her head towards the courtyard. "Have you heard something in the courtyard?" I got up and went to the bedroom window, opened a couple of Venetian blind slats and peered out. Nothing could be seen. I looked up at the archway, and then down towards the Priory kitchen. I couldn't see any movement at all. Nothing. I glanced down at my guys, and all three of them had rushed towards the bedroom door. "Okay, now you've all heard it haven't you?" I opened the door, and watched as they ran towards the large window seat. Jumping on it, all three heads turned towards me accusingly. *"Open it! Open the curtains now!"* I could almost hear them shouting at me in their heads. When I opened the curtain, they all as one looked towards the empty stable cottage that was used for storage. Standing behind them, I peered over their heads towards the stable door and windows. At first I saw nothing, but seeing their intent stares at it, I looked even harder. Then I saw it. Faint eddies of smoke rose from beneath the stable door, and in the stable window I could see tiny orange flickers. "Fire! The stables are on fire!" My pets all turned towards me. I could see what they were thinking. *"We told you so."*

I texted Jim, Martin and Tenby, then I rushed back to my bedroom. I threw jeans and a sweatshirt on. "Okay guys, well spotted, you watch from the windows, I'm going out now!" By this time loud angry voices were coming from the courtyard. I knew my text alerts had roused all the men. They were now taking action. Time I joined them!

***

The stable doors were wide open. Jim, stood with Martin beside him. The angry swearing and shouting came from

Sam. I'd forgotten that he'd been sleeping in the empty cottage after he'd worked late on his furniture restoration. Sam was now walking up and down, angry jerky movements engulfed his whole body. Rage consumed him. When he saw me coming towards him, he could only point. I followed that finger and could only stare appalled. The true love, and only love of Sam's life lay on its side on the stable floor. A fire had been set beside it and the flames had obviously caused some damage. I could see the kindling and paper that had been set on fire beside the bike had been kicked away. That was obviously Sam, I thought. There was damage from the fire, but it could have been so much worse. Flora, and her nose and ear for danger had saved Sam's motorcycle from complete destruction.

"Torched! Only my bike! Nothing else has been touched. Only my bike! How the hell was my bike a threat to someone. Who torched it? And why?"

Tenby had joined us now and stood looking down at the sorry spectacle of Sam's bike. "Leave it all now. Lock everything up and I'll get someone to look at it tomorrow."

"Come on Sam, I'll put the coffee pot on," said Maggie, who had heard all the fuss, and had joined us from her apartment in the Priory House. "Back to the kitchen. We all need a hot drink and maybe something extra in it."

"She's right Sam," I placed a hand on the tattooed muscular arm that was still shaking. "Let's have a hot drink and sort out a plan of action. This has got to stop, we can't sit by and let this sort of vandalism keep on happening."

Somehow no one wanted to be the first to leave the dreadful scene. That tragic sight of Sam's beloved motorcycle almost destroyed by fire had us all mesmerized.

"What's it all about? It's all just meaningless vandalism," said Martin.

"No it's not," I said with quiet certainty. "It's not meaningless. There is a definite pattern and reasoning behind it." I had been certain that I had seen the pattern behind these acts of violence towards us, but still unsure of my theory, I hadn't really wanted to explain it to the others, not yet, not without better facts and evidence. I could be so wrong. What if my theory was just idiotic and stupid.

"Let's hear it Daisy," said Sam.

"My pets are my great love. Your motorbike Sam is very important to you. Each and every one of us has been targeted in some degree, to cause us the most distress and fear. I think that's happened in the village. That's my theory, for what it's worth."

"Damn good theory Daisy," said Tenby with an approving nod towards me. "You are correct, there have been strange incidents in the village, where treasured possessions have been vandalised.

"Come on! To the kitchen and out of the cold. Sam, stop staring at your bike, if it can be repaired it will be. If not, the insurance will buy you something new." Maggie was having no nonsense from any of us. Angry barking from my cottage was echoed by anxious ones from Maisie in the Priory kitchen. "Daisy, bring your pets to the kitchen. The animals are hyped up with all the goings-on out here, they can run round there together."

Coffee with a dash of whisky, or brandy, and scalding hot tea for me was drunk with appreciation. The panic, the actual fire itself and the targeted evil at us as individuals, had shocked each one of us.

"Someone knows each one of us as individuals extremely well," murmured Jim. There were nods of agreement. "This blackmailer knows everyone in the village and all their secrets. All the letters that Roy steamed open must have finished. This blackmailer is making either general type guesses, or he knows stuff about the villagers," Jim added, still deep in thought.

"What other attempts on people in the village have there been? Have there been many?" I asked.

"Yes, Daisy, there have been other incidents in the village. Susan's cat had green paint thrown on him. John Tomlinson built a bar in his garden, it took many hours, and he was thrilled with the result. That mysteriously burnt down last week. Peggy who lives near to the post office had her magnolia tree chopped down, just as it was beginning to flower. She was heartbroken when she found it. There have been other incidents, but I haven't heard of any details about them. Those incidents were put down to kids, or unfortunate mishaps," Maggie told us.

"It's someone in the village, or they wouldn't know about these things. They seem to have picked objects, pets and things that are important to the owners. It's someone with a spiteful vengeful streak," Martin said with a shudder.

"Two murders, the attack on Hilda and numerous incidents and damage, but why? What's the reason behind it all? If it was just money from the blackmail, but it's not. The blackmail is something else. Is this being done by two different people, or just one?" Maggie asked as she got up to offer everyone another shot of whisky or brandy in their coffee.

Jim looked up from his coffee mug and spoke quietly. "There is a vindictive hatred behind all these actions. A hatred towards the Priory, and everyone in the village. Evil consumes this person. We have an evil killer stalking the village and the Priory!"

CHAPTER THIRTY-SIX

Another parcel arrived next morning. This time it was for Martin. It wasn't a goldfish, which we had got used to arriving, and were expecting. No, it was a haddock fillet! His secret was to be revealed if he didn't drop the money off that afternoon, again at the loose stone behind the litter bin in the car park at four o'clock.

"I haven't got a secret! What does he mean? What secret, I haven't got any secrets." Martin sat at the kitchen table, hands waving in denial and despair. The hands stopped suddenly when he realised we were all laughing. "Why are you laughing? What's so funny?"

"Of course you haven't got any secrets Martin. We know you haven't," Maggie tried to soothe the flustered Martin. "It's just you of all people getting a blackmail letter, and not even with a goldfish. You got a haddock fillet!"

The smiles from each one of us drew an answering smile from Martin, and he sat straighter on his chair. "Okay, I suppose I was silly getting so het up. But when you see your name written like that in the green ink, it throws you."

"Ha! So successful at it yesterday, he's even playing the same trick again. We can't let him or her escape us this time. There must be some way to foil his plan." Sheila declared. She was back from babysitting duties, and had been brought up to date with the ongoing activities of the blackmailer. Sheila was fired up with enthusiasm, and was waving her Agenda book around gleefully as she started plotting.

"I'll leave you all to the planning, hope you find something that will stop this blackmailer in his tracks. I've got to go and see my mother," I said.

"How is it all working out with your mother?" Sheila asked me. They had all been involved in my successful attempt to search for my birth mother and family. Sheila especially felt that she had a proprietorial interest in my family affairs.

"Okay, she's full of interest for Jake, her grandson. There's no problem with him. Sometimes she is great with me, other times I find her staring at me in a peculiar fashion. I wish I knew what she was thinking, and what it meant." I stood at the door, awkwardly, endlessly twisting my hands together. "It's so strange, she's so like my adoptive mum, she would be, because after all they were sisters. Yet sometimes she's so very different, and I find myself feeling off balance with her and her unexpected remarks."

"It's to be expected Daisy. You both have lifetimes of living apart. You didn't know of her existence at all. But remember you were her child, she must have thought about you often. Blood does not make us close to each other automatically. It may well take time," said Sheila.

I nodded and smiled at her as I made to leave. What could I say? She was right in so many ways. The only problem was my mother's great age. There may not be much time left I thought.

***

The van was already packed with my latest paintings. Carefully wrapped, they were in the back ready for my visit to the art shop and Jeff. Deliberately arranged by me to follow on from my mother's visit, it added an enjoyable aspect to my day. Jeff's cheerful chatting, and harmless mock flirting always cheered me up. Today was going to be special he told me yesterday on the phone. "I've got a great idea, but it will depend on your cooperation. I won't be able to do it without your agreement."

"So, there's no pressure on me," I said in reply. "Can you give me a hint of what it's about?" It hadn't worked, no hints were forthcoming. Wondering what it could be, kept away the nervousness that always came when I visited my mother in the care home.

***

The van door was locked, my precious paintings covered with a rug, I pulled my jacket down, patted my hair, and prepared to enter the care home. The box that she'd given to me on my last visit, still lay unopened in the bedroom top cupboard. I hoped that she wouldn't remember giving it to me. Maybe she wouldn't mention it at all.

"She's fine today, but don't stay too long. Yesterday she became very tired. There were a couple of phone calls, and one upset her." The carer whispered to me as I walked into the room. I placed my tin of Maggie's chocolate chip cookies on the small table beside her, removing the empty tin, and popping it into my bag.

"I do love those cookies, they are the best I've ever tasted," my mother said.

"Yes, they're too good. It's a struggle to keep my weight down with such great cooking from Maggie every day," I smiled at her.

Absentmindedly she nodded at me. There was silence. I didn't speak, because I could see that she had something on her mind. A couple of times she glanced at me, began to speak, then changed her mind and looked away. Unable to bear the silence, I began to talk about the weather, and the plants that I had bought for my new garden. My Mother smiled at these remarks, although I knew she wasn't listening to me with her full attention.

Those thoughts occupying her mind were of greater importance. As I looked at her again, a single tear found its way down the wrinkled cheek. She lifted her frail hand and brushed it away, then she reached for a tissue. I waited. She took a deep breath, and the same hand that wiped the tears away reached out to grasp mine. For all its fragility my hand was held in a vice-like grip.

"I had news yesterday, sad news. Someone I loved dearly passed away." I made as if to speak, but she shook my hand, and shushed me to silence. "He had been ill for some time and had lapsed into a coma. In some ways it was a relief and a blessing that he passed on. No one would wish him to continue in that state." I didn't speak, but nodded agreement. She sipped at tea which the carer had obviously just brought into her. I opened the tin and placed a chocolate chip cookie on the plate, pushing the shop bought Digestives to one side. She placed the teacup upon the saucer with great care. "He was the only man I have loved. Both you and Violet were born out of a great love, never forget that. I'm explaining this to you Daisy, because I don't think you will condemn us. Violet has led a narrow existence here in Cornwall. She never wanted to leave home, she had an office job locally, and never seemed at all adventurous. Unlike you, she has never experienced the world, the people that inhabit it, and how our moral life and boundaries can sometimes be blurred. Violet has strange straitlaced ideas and would possibly be shocked, whereas I think you will be understanding and sympathetic." Another sip of the tea, and she sank back into her pillows. That long speech and its depth of meaning had exhausted her. In the silence, my thoughts were swirling around in my head.

I sat motionless. Even when the carer brought in a mug of tea for me, I could only smile and thank her wordlessly. What was coming? I felt that my mother was on the edge giving me some life changing revelation. Was this about my father? I thought it must be, she mentioned that Violet and I had been born out of love. I sipped the tea. It was far too strong for me, not like my usual dishwater. But I drank it and enjoyed the harsh bitterness of the tannin on my tongue. It brought reality to my mind; it took me away from the here and the now of this difficult situation.

Straightening up, she rallied and began to speak clearly and deliberately, never taking her eyes off my face. "He was married when we met, but she was very ill. Nowadays she would have had treatment, but then… They sent her off for long periods into an asylum. Then they gave her electric shock treatment, several times she endured it. It somehow destroyed the essence of her personality, and she was never the same again. We both loved her; she had been my great friend through childhood. He loved her in his fashion, we both did, but this was not the person that we had once known. Never think that we didn't love, care or look after her. We both did. Looking after her and spending so much time together it was inevitable that we grew closer. Then I gave birth to a son."

"A son? Violet and I have a brother?" I think the words came out as a high-pitched squeak.

My mother ignored my comment, and took another sip of tea. Again she placed her cup with infinite care upon the saucer. I wanted to tell her to hurry up, tell me more about this brother I had. "It was decided that the boy should remain with his father, and we passed him off as their child. It was easy. She was away so much for various treatments, it could have been that she had borne the child on one of these long visits. Then you and Violet were born. This time I was going to have the girls, but my sister was barren and could have no children. On the condition that they lived nearby, and both girls grew up as close cousins, I gave you to her. When she took you away, a piece of my heart went with you. I never forgave her you know. Never."

The rustle of the pillows behind her as she sank back against them were the only sound in the room. The soft-spoken words from my mother had left me bewildered and unable to comprehend the words that she was saying. Their meaning and the information she was giving was hard to grasp and accept. Outside her room I could hear voices and footsteps along the corridor. Life was going on as normal in the care home. But not in this room. Those few remarks from my mother had changed my life. The smell of her lavender perfume seemed to enfold me in a cloud of her remembrances. Those words telling me of her past had caused a seismic change in my life, and that of my sister. I needed to know more. I bent forward, the questions rising to my lips.

The bustle of the carer behind me startled me. I had been so intent on listening to my Mother's revelations. "I think your mother has done too much talking. She needs to rest now." She stepped forward to straighten my mother's pillows. There was a speaking look directed towards me. I realised I was being told to leave.

"You understand Daisy? I was certain you would understand and forgive." The whisper was faint as she lay further back onto the pillows. Her hand pressed mine in supplication now, and her eyes searched my face anxiously.

"Of course I understand, and there is nothing to forgive. We were all born out of love and that is all that matters," I whispered to her. Her face glowed with an inner relief and calm at my words. I meant every one of them, and she realised that. I could see that, and the agitated look faded away, and she drifted off to sleep.

***

I don't remember getting into my van. I must have left my mother's room in a daze. There were so many questions I had wanted to ask her. Who was the father? He'd obviously just died so there was no hope of Violet ever meeting him. I knew she'd be upset. But we had a brother! An older brother! That was something to investigate now. If only I could have got more out of my mother. If only that carer had not appeared. My mother told me the story, explained why they did it, and what happened to the babies. But not a name! No places mentioned. Apart from hearing about this brother, I was no further forward in our search for the father we had never known. I had a brother!

CHAPTER THIRTY-SEVEN

Demelza came into the Priory kitchen, just as we were finishing breakfast. Accompanying her was a dark-haired young woman in her early thirties. Her deep-set eyes flicked around the kitchen, widening at the stone pillars and archways. "I'm useless to you all with his arm in plaster. Leah can help us out. She's Annie's daughter. The gift shop she was working in has closed down, the owner retired. Whilst she is looking for another job I suggested that she fill in for me."

"That's great Demelza," Maggie went over to the woman with an outstretched hand. Hesitating for a moment Leah shook her hand and muttered something under her breath.

Jim looked at me and raised an eyebrow. I shrugged my shoulders, but I felt an unpleasant vibe about the woman. Then I rebuked myself. A few moments, and I was already making a snap judgement. It's got to stop Daisy, I told myself, she may be a pleasant girl, just nervous and shy. That's it, I told myself firmly, she's nervous and shy.

"What will you be doing in the meantime Demelza?" Sheila asked her.

A faint flush ran up Demelza's neck and face. "I'm helping Sam and Gerald out. They are clearing one of the barns on their property. It's going to be an office for the online renovated furniture business. It has a separate driveway onto the road, completely separate from the cottage, so it could also be used as a shop in the future."

"You're not moving stuff or painting walls with that arm, are you?" Sheila was alarmed at the prospect of Demelza in action with her arm in plaster.

"No!" Demelza laughed at Sheila's horrified look.

"No, I'm strictly project manager. I will decide where the office will go, how to display furniture for online sales etc. I shall enjoy it, bossing those two about should be fun!"

"Thank goodness, for a moment you had me worried there," Sheila said.

"Whilst I do that Leah has a breathing space to sort out her future plans," Demelza smiled at the woman who nodded at her. The lank brown hair cut in a straight line to chin length fell forward hiding her face.

"What would you like to do? Have you any plans?" Sheila always inquisitive, asked the young woman.

The hair was tossed back as Leah looked at Sheila. "I'm not sure. I think I'd like to work in an office, and become an estate agent just like my cousin Francesca."

"Francesca? Is that Frankie that works for the local estate agent?" Jim asked.

"Yes, she's my cousin."

"Well Leah, if you need any time off for interviews, don't hesitate to ask me," Maggie told her.

I noted the look of surprise that crossed Leah's face. Why was she so astonished that Maggie should be nice to her?

***

Jim and I left the kitchen together. When we walked into the courtyard he looked at me. "I'm thinking of talking to Gerald, would you like to come with me and see what they're doing at their cottage?" I knew better than to ask Jim what he wanted to talk to Gerald about. If Jim wanted me to know he would tell me. I was also very curious to see what Demelza and the two guys were up to, so I readily agreed. Jim reached into his pocket for his phone.

"Hi Gerald, are you at the cottage? Can you spare me

a few minutes? Can Daisy and I come over for a chat?" We walked to Jim's cottage door. "Okay, you are stopping for lunch anyway sometime soon. I have to tell Daisy to bring Lottie and Flora, the garden is perfectly safe for them. They're ordering a takeaway. Will pizza do you Daisy? You know how Gerald will only eat a pizza takeaway" Jim folded up his phone and walked towards my cottage with me. I knew that my dogs would love to go out for a visit to somewhere new. I only hoped that they would behave. As I got them ready with harnesses, and put them safely into the back of my van, Jim stood looking miserable.

"What's the matter?" I asked him.

"This is not what I wanted. I hoped for a quiet word with Gerald about some puzzling research on the Knights Templars. This sounds as if it's going to be a party, there'll be no chance for a serious discussion." He shook his head, then wandered round and climbed into the passenger seat.

"Don't be so dramatic Jim! A serious discussion can take place after the pizza party. You and Gerald can go off somewhere quiet to discuss your problem."

Jim's body stiffened, and his face set into hard lines. Then he looked at me and began to laugh. "Was I getting a little dramatic? Perhaps you're right I do tend to dramatise things a little."

"A little!" I replied, and the laughter between us helped clear the air and lessen the tension that had been building up in Jim.

***

We drove along a part of Bodmin Moor that was new to me. This long stretch of moorland was of a higher elevation than the village and Priory. It stretched into the distance on either side of the road with little sign of trees or habitation. It was an eerie landscape and felt otherwordly. I realised that we were not that far from Jamaica Inn. I could understand the role that smugglers had played in that story, and the isolation that helped keep their secrets. The road began to wind down into a valley, and we drove alongside the river that gurgled its way between trees and the road itself. A few cottages and a farmhouse set back from the road were the only habitation we saw.

"Not far now, it's just around this bend," said Jim.

I slowed down and became aware of the stone cottage on my left. It was large, and long, and looked extremely old.

"Go past this drive, Daisy. This leads up to the barn, we go into the next drive which leads up to the cottage."

I got out of the van, and stretched, stiff from the drive, before I turned to the dogs in the back. They were excited and looked out of the window, tails wagging furiously. "What a lovely cottage, and such a wonderful position. No wonder Gerald didn't want to sell it," I enthused. The windows looked out across the valley, whilst the river had crossed under the road and could be seen chuckling along on the other side. The sloping hills behind the cottage obviously gave it shelter from the prevailing winter winds. Freshly painted, with the garden neatly kept with the promise of an abundant flower crop in the summer, it all showed Gerald's handiwork.

The door opened as we walked up to it. "Come in! Come on Flora and Lottie, you will love our garden." Gerald held the door back, and waved the dogs through the hall and out the kitchen door which was open to the garden. "They'll be perfectly safe out there, my father had a dog, so the garden was secured for it."

"Thanks Gerald, what a lovely place you have here.

No wonder you didn't want to leave. I'm sure the dogs will love exploring, a new place with lots of exciting smells will be wonderful for them."

"We have to talk Gerald, I must talk to you," Jim said, grasping Gerald's arm in his agitation.

"Let's get in first Jim, it will wait until we've all said hello." I snapped at him. I understood and sympathized with him, but felt it needed to be put into perspective.

"Okay, okay, you are right. It will wait until Gerald has a free moment," grumbled Jim.

I walked into the oak panelled hall. It opened out into the kitchen through which the garden could be seen. As I paused, the doorbell rang behind us. Jim, who was standing beside me, had his hand in a flash behind his back at his waistband. He caught my eye and dropped the hand with a sheepish expression. Sheila would have said that Jim was packing, and ready for action. The doorbell gave another loud ring.

A voice called through the open front door. "Pizza delivery!"

Jim's hand had fallen to his side, and he followed me still wearing that sheepish expression. Unusually for Jim, he was so unsettled by the latest murders, attacks and surveillance upon him, he was acting without any conscious thought.

Excited snuffles and barks from Lottie and Flora came from the kitchen. I followed them and laughed when I saw their excitement. Demelza who had just arrived before us, and Sam were setting out condiments and cutlery on the large oak kitchen table. To my surprise, and I was still uncertain about how I felt about it, both my pets adored Sam. Demelza was their friend of long-standing. Sam had erupted into their doggy lives, playing ridiculous games on the floor with them, and he had now become their very special friend.

"Come and see the barn Daisy. I've had a great idea for you, come on!" Demelza grabbed my arm with her good one, and guided me through a door from the kitchen into a corridor with a door at the end. Flinging it wide-open she said, "Ta Da!" and gestured me inside. I stepped through and looked around openmouthed. It was a vast space. Stone walls and huge wooden trusses held up the barn roof. At one end was Sam's working area, with finished projects, some half-done ones, and piled in a corner were sad furniture wrecks awaiting his care and expertise. Pulling me yet further into the barn, Demelza waved her good arm. "Look Daisy, I've got a wonderful idea for you. Look over there!"

CHAPTER THIRTY-EIGHT

"Your paintings can go there! Some in front of this velvet curtain that I have hung up over part of the wall. We'll do a group against the stone walls, to soften the look of the stone. They'll be a backdrop to Sam's renovated furniture. I'm sure we'll sell loads of your paintings online. Won't that be great? I'm absolutely certain that we'll sell every single one of your paintings, and fast!"

Demelza was excited for me. Her enthusiasm was almost overpowering me. Almost! I smiled at her, but inwardly my heart sank. My painting was my refuge, my relaxation time. I enjoyed it, especially my flowers and vegetables. Churning them out was not something I wanted to do. All the pleasure would be taken from my paintings. Demelza didn't realise that botanical art could not be rushed. She was in a bright happy zone. I couldn't burst her bubble of happiness, especially as she still suffered from the after-effects of Jason's beating. We could always take prints from my work I thought to myself. "Wonderful, the velvet curtain against the stonework looks stunning." It was a weak remark, but she didn't seem to notice and smiled happily at me.

Gerald joined us, his delight in this new enterprise was obvious, his cheerful demeanor and excited remarks made that apparent. "Thank you Daisy. Your idea has brought this old cottage to life. We are all involved in this venture, it's hard work but so enjoyable. Thank you!" To his own astonishment and definitely to mine, Gerald hugged me, and kissed me on the cheek. "I've been sent to get you both, Jim and Sam have sorted out drinks and pizzas in the kitchen, you've to come in and get them."

Laughter and further ideas and plans mingled together as the new business was discussed. Jim joined in occasionally, but I could tell that he was still dwelling on that stone that had appeared mysteriously on his dining table.

***

The meal was finished, and we went into the lounge. Old beams and stone walls gave the room an antiquity which was offset by neutral paint work, exquisite antiques and huge squashy sofas facing the cream log burner. My eye was caught by the armchairs either side of the fire. Maps and Knights Templar books, all concerning Cornwall were piled up on a table beside one chair. That had to be Gerald's chair. The other armchair had a table beside it, again piled up with books. Those books left me gob smacked, as I twisted my head to see the writing on their spines. Sam's tough exterior gave the impression of a musclebound guy with little intellect or brain. Antique books on furniture were to be expected as he was involved with his furniture restoration. But it had been the other pile of books that left me surprised. Dostoevsky, Dick Francis and Hemingway had been amongst other classic authors that I glimpsed when I walked past.

We settled down and relaxed. It was Sam who spoke first. "Come on Jim, out with it," said Sam. "You might as well tell us. If you don't you may well explode with what's worrying you."

We all laughed at that remark and even Jim managed a faint smile. Jim looked me and I nodded my agreement to Sam's suggestion. "Okay Sam. You win. I would prefer that this is kept between us, the fewer people who know the better."

There were nods of agreement and Sam said, "of course Jim. You know we can all keep secrets, we've done it before."

"A few days ago," began Jim and explained about the Watcher and his surveillance. How little headway Jim had made in both stopping the guy, filming him, or finding out his identity rankled with him. It showed in his telling the tale,

"That's when I saw you find a bug in your car, I also noticed you put up extra cameras," said Sam.

"You saw them! I thought I'd hidden them," exclaimed a horrified Jim.

"They were well hidden, let's just say my past days in the Army... And leave it at that. Don't worry Jim, they are extremely well hidden." Sam grinned at the expression on all our faces.

Silence fell on the room. Each one of us stared at Sam. Who was this guy? And what exactly had he done in the army? Had we got another spy amongst us? Surely not! I didn't believe in coincidences, but..."

Jim rallied first, a shrewd look at Sam, an acknowledgement of his remarks and he got out his phone. "Today when I got home I went into my cottage. Not only had someone been in there, but they left me something. It was a large stone with a sign written upon it." Flicking through the photos on this phone, he found the one and passed it around. "Have a look."

Sam looked at it, shook his head and passed it to Demelza. Again, that shake of her head, and it was passed to Gerald. "Oh yes! I know what this is!"

CHAPTER THIRTY-NINE

Gerald looked up from the phone. All eyes were upon him, and each one of us were awaiting a pronouncement from him. "It's a drawing on a stone of the Hooked X." He sat back to await our intelligent comments. There were none. Still we stared at him.

"What's the Hooked X?" Sam asked.

Ignoring his brother, Gerald turned to Jim. "Don't you recognise it? I thought you would know it immediately you saw it."

"I thought I recognised it. But not in the context you mean. I was so convinced it was someone from my past work life, I completely disregarded the link to the Templars," Jim said.

"Ah! The good old spy days," laughed Sam.

Jim gave a start of surprise, and his appalled recognition at Sam's remark gave his secret away. It wasn't really a secret, we had all guessed previously what his civil service job entailed.

"That's what Sam was! He was something like that in the army. Fancy that, both of you being some sort of spy. That's an amazing coincidence," said Gerald.

"Daisy doesn't believe in coincidences," muttered Jim. He was slowly coming back from his surprise. I was gazing at Sam with a dawning respect.

"Never mind about your past occupations, you can both chat about them later. What is this X thingy? Gerald, what does leaving a stone in the middle of the table with a Hooked X sign on it mean?" Demelza asked impatiently.

Gerald sat back for a moment and thought before he spoke. "It's difficult to explain, but think of the Da Vinci code," he began saying.

"Not those crackpots again!" Jim exploded, and began pacing around the room. The lounge here was much bigger than my kitchen and lounge, so he had much more room to pace about. "Thank goodness I showed it to you Gerald. You may well be right. I never thought of them. I had trouble with them before. Don't you remember Daisy? They thought I was investigating their family links to the Templars. I wasn't, and once I told them that they backed off."

"But how does this stone tell you all this?" Demelza asked Gerald.

Gerald sat back in his armchair, his two fingers enlarging the stone. "Can you see that the cross has a line jutting out of the top of one of the crosses. It's meant to signify Jesus, and Mary Magdalen. It's a sign the Templars used, that's what some people believe."

"What's that sign doing on a stone in the middle of Jim's cottage table?" I demanded.

"It's a puzzle, there is no mistaking that," murmured Demelza.

"Where does that sign come from originally? And why go to the trouble of finding a stone the right size and shape, and then putting this mark on it especially for Jim to find?" I said.

"I think you're right Jim, it's those people that contacted us before, that's when Sam and I..." Gerald went beetroot red, as he remembered Sam's attacks on us in the past. The past. That was the fact I had to remember; it was all in the past. Sam had promised to turn over a new leaf, and never to cause any more trouble. He seemed to be keeping that promise. It would take a lot for me to forgive and forget, forgive maybe, forgetting was another matter entirely!

"Yes, you're right Gerald. There was someone who contacted me very politely and asked how the research was going. A pleasant spoken man told me to keep to a certain path in my research. As I didn't touch on any hereditary Templar families, the conversation ended amicably. Why now? Why are they contacting me now? Is it the same guys?" Jim demanded looking around at us all.

Blank faces greeted these questions, not one of us knew the answer to any one of those questions. Not one of us was stupid enough to pass one silly placating remark to Jim. We could all tell that he was on a short fuse.

"Send me the photo Jim. I'll look out any links that I can find tonight," said Gerald.

"You thought this sophisticated hardware used to watch you could only be ex-military or government. Could these Templar fanatics have the ability and gear to search and watch your cottage in such a high-tech manner?" I asked Jim.

"I don't know. I can't work it out. This Templar's stone thing adds another puzzlingly layer to an already bizarre situation," answered Jim.

"Okay, I'm coming back with you two. Jim and I can bed down in his cottage tonight. You Jim will go in your front door as you usually do. I will sneak in hopefully unobserved through the back. Let's have someone sitting waiting for the Watchers next visit!"

Jim said the usual things, that he could manage, didn't want to bother Sam, and so on. He was overruled by everyone of us, and I could tell that he was actually delighted about it. Sam had been a formidable enemy and there were obvious advantages in having him on our side.

Lottie and Flora were exhausted. A new garden and house to explore were exciting. Best of all in their eyes, was that this new place included some of their favourite people. Sam provided games and fun, and they adored his antics with them. Demelza had always provided them with treats and cuddles. But they were getting anxious now. Were they going to stay here and miss out on their dinner? Anxious faces were being turned towards me, and still I sat in the armchair. Gerald delved into his bookshelves with the eager help of Jim. I heard mumbles about rune stones, Christopher Columbus signature, and Rosslyn Abbey. Sam was upstairs packing an overnight bag, and I helped Demelza clear the pizza and dinner plates.

"Your bruises have nearly gone now, there's just a faint yellow tinge left. Have you heard any more about Jason?"

Demelza placed the tea towel back on its rail and turned to smile at me. "I've not heard from him, but I heard from his mother!"

"What? His mother?" I gasped. Her mother-in-law had always accused her of making Jason's attacks up, believing her son whenever he swore innocence.

"Somehow all my hospital injury photos, and the medical report on my injuries found their way to her and all his friends. I don't know how they were sent." Demelza began to laugh. "We, you and I, have another family member who works in the hospital. Those injury photos and the report were somehow copied and sent by them."

"This is some family I have found myself part of! I think I'm going to enjoy being part of this family. So what did Jason's mother say?" I said, eager to hear more.

"She sent me a bunch of flowers with an apology. Best of all, she paid Jason's airfare to join his brother and to work in his bar. She said it was a one-way ticket, there was no return! Then I got more flowers, another couple of bouquets. The delivery girl asked if it was my birthday."

"Who were they from?"

"From his mates! Apologies all round. They did not realise the extent of his violent abuse towards me. They also asked me to pass on their best wishes to the fat little person who broke his nose with a dustbin lid!" Demelza was by this time clutching her sides, whooping with laughter when the men walked into the kitchen.

"What's so funny?" Jim asked.

"Yes, come on share the joke." Sam said.

The story was told. Everyone laughed uproariously. I took the dogs out for a last trot around the garden. Even at the bottom of the garden I could hear the laughter!

CHAPTER FORTY

We drove back up the lane, dropping Sam off at a shady wooded section. His plan was to sneak up through the woods, over the fences and walls, keeping well away from the hidden cameras. Jim would have a window open ready for his entry.

***

The text came after an evening meal. A chicken casserole, everyone's favourite, had been left in the oven by Maggie whilst she'd been out. Over the meal, Jim had explained at great length the terrible pressure that he had been under, caused by the surveillance of the Watcher. Telling Gerald, Sam and Demelza had been cathartic in some way, so Jim was determined to go further down that route with the others. He was not disappointed, Maggie, Sheila and Martin made all the correct remarks and noises. So much so, Jim explained yet again in length. It may have relaxed him, but I was getting really fed up with it all!

Maggie was fidgeting, and to my eyes was waiting impatiently for Jim to finish his story. She had news, I could sense it. But like Maggie, I didn't interrupt Jim's flow of words. There was a visible lessening of tension in his face. That was a good sign, and if I had to put up with several minutes of the Watcher's prowess with surveillance techniques I would continue to do so. Finally he wound down, drank his coffee and sank back onto his chair exhausted.

"Maggie what's your news? I know you've got some." Every few minutes she had been looking at the phone and text. Since getting it, she had looked in turn confused and upset. I was beginning to worry. What was in that text to upset and worry her to such an extent? Maggie lifted her phone and waved it in the air. "The text is about Hilda Evans. Someone broke into the hospital and tried to kill her." At our concerned outcry, Maggie waved the phone again. "She's all right. A nurse came in and found the intruder trying to smother her. He pushed the nurse to one side and escaped."

"Who sent the text? When did it happen?" Jim wanted to know all the details.

"The text is from an old school friend, who knows of our interests. She was visiting someone down the corridor and heard all the commotion," Maggie replied.

"Hilda obviously knows something, and the killer doesn't want her to remember and tell. I thought she would only be a threat to Roy. She told us that she knew Roy's secret. What does she know about Roy's killer? The second killer must fear Hilda's knowledge of him!" Jim said thoughtfully.

"If only we could find out what she knew," I murmured partly to myself thinking out loud. I had been stirring my tea, another fresh cup and I looked up. Jim's eyes were fixed on me, and he had that look on his face. Oh no! Me and my big mouth, I should have kept that thought to myself. Jim's face had a dawning realisation of something, and my ill-advised words had set him off thinking. I didn't want to know. My bed was calling me, especially after a hot shower.

"Why can't we try to find out what Hilda knew? Shall we investigate?" Jim said. Only Martin had a doubtful look, Maggie and Sheila looked excited. You don't know what he has planned I thought. Neither did I, but I was certain it would be risky, possibly illegal.

***

Sometime later I got out of the SUV, and followed Maggie and Jim up to the cottage front door of Hilda Evans. Cold winds blew across my face, and not even my balaclava could keep the chill from it. I shivered; my ancient jacket was no match for the cold night air at two o'clock on Bodmin Moor. On our earlier visit to Hilda's cottage when we had been selling raffle tickets, it had been a bright sunny morning. Sunshine had invested that scene with a cheerful spring air, hinting at the promise of warmer weather. I shivered again. My jacket was dark blue, the only one suitable for burglary that I possessed. My outerwear had been chosen without the thought of investigating or burglary. The manufacturer said it was multipurpose, but I don't think this was what they had in mind. This coat I had used for dog walking, and early morning outings in the garden with the pets, not intending it for nefarious purposes. Sheila remained at the Priory manning the telephones in the kitchen, and had promised to have hot drinks ready on our return. Martin was in the SUV on watch duty, and as our getaway driver. Jim turned away from the front door and walked down the side path. Maggie and I followed Jim, as usual, until we reached the back door. I remembered, and I'm certain that Maggie and Jim also remembered another break-in when we acted upon Jim's instructions. That had been followed by an explosion. I shivered this time, but it wasn't from the cold. Our pinpoint torches held down to secure us a safe footing, had been grudgingly agreed to by Jim. Maggie and I had thought that it essential for us oldies.

Efficient as always, Jim's few seconds at the back door had it swing open. No burglar alarm, Maggie had already checked that with a friend. Maggie's network of friends in the village and the area was numerous, and could be counted on for information and help in the most peculiar of circumstances. And they never ever asked her awkward questions. "I'll go downstairs, can you both do upstairs?"

Maggie's eyes glittered in the faint light from our torches through her balaclava. Even hidden from me, I knew that her face would be a mirror image of my own. Dislike for what we were doing, when the poor woman lay in a hospital bed. That mingled with the fear that we would be found out. Maggie followed me up the stairs and whispered to me. "What are we looking for? What do we do if we find anything?" I shook my head; I didn't know either.

**

A few minutes later the three of us stood together in the lounge. "Nothing." Jim's shoulders had slumped in disappointment. "I don't even know what we should be looking for. I had hoped we might have found something."

There were sticky notes and a diary on a pretty antique desk. I walked over to give them a further look. All was neat and tidy. Antique pieces mixed in with comfortable modern armchairs. The kitchen was newly fitted with gleaming appliances, granite worktops and sparkling white units. There was an eclectic mix of old and new throughout the cottage, which gave it a cheerful friendly air, and I felt sorry for the woman so cruelly attacked. As I thought of her lying in the hospital bed, possibly still unconscious and in danger, I bowed my head and said a short prayer for her. Flicking through the bills paid, and those that had arrived and were needing paid I found nothing. I came across an old-fashioned account book, with careful methodical figures placed neatly and in order. I ran my finger down her last entries, and found a couple on the day of her attack. One name caught my eye. "That's it! I knew there was something familiar the moment we stepped into the cottage. It's the smell. Do you recognise it?" I asked the others.

"Yes I do! That's the polish Annie makes up herself to use on antique wood," Maggie replied, giving great big sniffs.

"She makes polish up herself? Surely not in this age of modern wonder cleaners," Jim said.

"Yes, she has a room at the back of her cottage. She makes polish, face creams and all sorts of herbal concoctions. Everyone walks through that room to reach her kitchen. Her garden is full of herbs and plants that she uses…" Maggie's voice faded away into silence. Then she spoke again. "You don't think Annie? Could she?" Silence filled the room.

"Annie's name is the last on this list." My pinpoint torch lit up Hilda's last entry for that day. *Don't forget to pay Annie this afternoon.*

Jim stepped forward and pointed to the entry. "It's not crossed off. Every other entry has been paid, and has been crossed off. Either Annie didn't come, or Hilda forgot to pay her, or cross it off the list."

"She was attacked before she had the chance to pay Annie, or…" I said.

"Not Annie! Surely you don't think Annie is the blackmailer and killer?" Maggie whispered. Despite her low voice, the words rang out as they painted a picture that not one of us wanted to see.

***

Sheila was waiting for us. She'd even got bacon sandwiches, and toasted cheese ready for us. And those sorely needed hot drinks.

"Thanks Sheila, it was so cold waiting outside, wondering what they were doing inside the cottage. When a couple of cars drove past I threw myself over the passenger seat…" Martin shuddered at the memory, before taking a huge bite of his bacon sandwich.

"Well? Don't keep me waiting in suspense! Did you find anything out?" Sheila demanded, after we had all sat down with our drinks and food.

"Not really Sheila, it was puzzling. The cottage seemed to hold no surprises or clues. Except for an account book Daisy found. Here it is Sheila, the entry that caused us to wonder what had happened," Jim passed his phone to Sheila, the relevant picture open, and then passed it to Martin.

"Annie? No, you can't think it's Annie. I've known her for years. Trustworthy, kind and helpful, that's Annie!" Sheila's reply was immediate.

"Annie has that room with all her herbs and potions, but she doesn't keep it locked. We walked straight into the kitchen that day we visited her. Anyone who goes there could have access to any of those ingredients she uses," I said.

"Good point," said Jim thoughtfully.

"So it needn't be Annie, it could be a visitor," said Sheila, relief flooding her voice.

"Who are her frequent visitors?" Jim said.

"Her daughter," Maggie started ticking each name off on her fingers. "Her daughter Leah of course, and Frankie her niece."

"Frankie! She could fit the profile we are looking for, she's got a Sicilian background, her father was from Sicily, and she is desperate for money to get to Exeter," Maggie said.

"Don't forget, Jasper said she was wearing an expensive watch, and was saving up for a deposit on a flat in Exeter. What about that charm we found? The one at the goldfish pond, that could be hers!" I said.

"It does all seem to fit," said Jim.

"I'd rather it was Francesca, she's an uppity girl. I don't want it to be Annie, I've known her for years and trust her. I'd hate to have my judgement proved wrong," said Sheila.

Jim rose to his feet. "That's possibly been more successful than I thought. It looks as if Francesca is now our number one suspect. Let's think about what we will do next after we sleep on it." His remark indicated that it was time for his bed. And we all agreed it, because it was well past our usual bedtime. Us oldies need an early night, even if we do wake at the crack of dawn.

***

As I got into bed, I thought of Francesca. I'd admired the girl's spirit and drive. She wanted to move to Exeter, but blamed her lack of money and her guilt at leaving her grandmother. What was true? Did she really want to move to Exeter? Surely if she'd been so desperate, she'd have found some way of getting there. As for blaming her grandmother, and saying that she needed her was a dubious reason. I'd heard that Frankie's grandmother was fit and even younger than me! It was all possibly an excuse. I thought that Frankie and her motives, her real motives needed further scrutiny. What was she hiding? Was it blackmail? Or was it murder?

CHAPTER FORTY-ONE

Sam had spent the night in Jim's spare bedroom. Nothing had transpired, and both men looked disappointed when they arrived for breakfast. I was delighted. My sleep had been patchy lately, broken with weird dreams and sudden starts. The blackmailer and the Watcher were anonymous, threatening figures. That made it worse. Our last adventure had villains, but we knew who they were. Their routines, their workplaces were all under our scrutiny. That meant we only had to prove their guilt. Only! It had been a difficult and frightening time. Yet this felt worse somehow. Skulking in shadows, anonymous behind their evil deeds. Who was it? That was a question that each and everybody was asking. That very anonymity was so disturbing.

The village atmosphere had changed. The former openness and trust between neighbour and friend had gone. Suspicion coloured every conversation, and curbs were kept upon tongues. Who knew if the person chatting to you was the blackmailer? Perhaps they were eager to learn more of your secret life? Even the puppy class had been strained, and they had not the usual happy fun with the dogs. Martin had complained to us. "They look at Maggie and I, and know that we are investigating. They don't chat normally with us. I think they're frightened that we will put them on the top of our suspect list. Others badger us for information, thinking that we must know the latest police details with Tenby living here. The last class was unpleasant, the dogs knew it, and they behaved badly."

Sheila placed the agenda book carefully beside her plate. Her face was drawn, and she moved with extreme care. Last night's excitement had been too much for our octogenarian. Her bubbly personality and cheerful manner hid the age-related ailments and her genetic complaints. Maggie gave her a searching look and glanced towards me. I nodded and she murmured, "later." We had to make certain that Sheila did less, whilst making her useful, and ensuring that she didn't realise our machinations.

The text alert came in for Maggie. "Hilda is out of danger now, but still unable to remember her attack. That's promising isn't it?"

Our visit to Hilda's house last night had brought the woman into sharper focus. Previously the raffle tickets we'd sold to her, and the conversation we'd had then with her, had been our only meeting.

"What's today's investigative tasks?" Sheila said. Today's date was not only written in her book but decorated with stars. Yesterday the date had been decorated with flowers. "Should we look for more goldfish ponds? Check out the drop-off point again? Or what? Any ideas?" There were no answers. Even Jim had run out of ideas to investigate.

"Nothing on today, no investigating ideas, nothing." Sheila closed her agenda book with a dramatic sigh and a bang. Silence. Everyone finished their breakfast, drank their coffee, but then sat in a despondent quiet.

"It's going to be a lovely day, the sun is shining," I said as I looked out of the window.

"I know what we'll do!" Maggie leapt to her feet and clapped her hands. "Let's take the day off."

Everyone jumped. Martin spluttered his coffee out over his muesli. Sheila's spoon clattered into her almost empty bowl startling us all still further.

"We've always got the day off, we're retired," Sheila said.

"Do you remember when we went to picnics at

Polzeath? Let's forget murderers, dead fish and blackmail. We should go out for the day!" Maggie's voice rose in excitement as she explained her idea to us.

"Picnic? Can we come too?" Sam stood in the doorway with Gerald. Both had similar expressions on their faces. Neither of them wanted to be left out of what promised to be a fun day.

"Good idea Maggie. We're all jaded and living on top of the problems. A day out will clear our heads..." Jim was saying when Sheila interrupted him.

"We'll recharge our batteries, and be newly invigorated to begin again with the investigation." Excitement had swept over Sheila's whole body, and she was bouncing up and down in her chair in delight. Her grandkids, Ben and Rosie seemed at times more adult than Sheila ever did!

"Where will we go? We're not fit enough to warrant beach walks. What about the dogs? When we went to the beach before, we had no dogs." I said, thinking of the practical logistics.

"Lanhydrock! That's where we'll go. Lots of space for dog walks. The house and gorgeous gift shop to explore out of the cold wind. The outdoor café in the courtyard is where we can sit and have our lunch with the dogs," said Maggie.

"That sounds great. When shall we go?" I asked Maggie.

"Now! Let's get ready and go right now," said Maggie.

***

We took the SUV and my van. The dogs were strapped in the back of the SUV altogether. Maisie was joining the pups this time. I'll swear little Maisie was grinning broadly. She was so used to seeing the other two go off to puppy class without her. Jim joined me in the van, the others piled into the SUV. Sheila was going to potter around the house and gift shop, "There are places where I can sit, and then I'll join you all outside for lunch," she told us. The journey through the countryside was stunning. Cornwall is atmospheric and beautiful throughout the year. But it's in Spring she possesses an entrancing magical beauty. Trees bud earlier, bulbs pop out of the earth with a colour, and freshness not seen in any other part of the United Kingdom.

***

The buggy was available for Sheila from the gate to the house. The dogs were super excited, all of us together, and a strange new smelly walk. At the house entrance we split up. The guys went off with the dogs whilst we joined Sheila at the house entrance.

"I love the old kitchens," said Demelza. "When I go and look at the utensils and the pans they used, I thank my lucky stars that I don't live in the past."

"It's the clothes washing and ironing that seemed so time-consuming and backbreaking," I said as we investigated the laundry artefacts.

"If you were born above stairs, you'd never realise the hard work your servants did. I'll bet some of the great ladies never once ventured into their own kitchens," said Sheila thoughtfully.

"I think it would have been a different sort of servitude. Forced to sit and conform to the rules and standards of the day. Boredom must have been a constant in their lives," I said.

Our musings upon the way of life of our ancestors came to an abrupt halt when we reached the gift shop.

Solitary missions to purchase were undertaken by each one of us. Immersed in shopping it was with a sudden coming up for air that our purchases were paid for, placed in bags, and we exited the gift shop. So many delightful local products had caught our attention, books about the local area, ornaments and gifts made in Cornwall, they were all so tempting. Bright sunlight had us all blinking, or was it reaction from our retail shopping therapy? Walking out of the gift shop we turned towards the courtyard and its café.

"I want to look around the formal garden later. After a sit down with my lunch, maybe I can manage it," said Sheila.

Maggie looked doubtfully at me and shook her head. Sheila's enthusiastic shopping for tea towels, Cornish novels, and Cornish honey, had meant that she'd been on her feet far longer than was good for her.

***

The men and dogs were already seated when we went round the corner. Excited jumping about, barking and general mayhem greeted our arrival from the dogs. "They have had a long walk, you'd have thought they would have been too tired to cause this commotion," said Jim shaking his head at their exuberance. Sam, Gerald and Maggie went up to order for us all, bringing back teas and coffees.

"This is great," said Sheila, smiling up at Maggie she placed a coffee in front of her. "It was a marvelous idea."

"I agree, it has been such a welcome change of scene. Well done Maggie," said Jim.

Pasties, sausage rolls, and sandwiches with crusty artisan bread were eaten in silence. A constant bustle around us of people coming and going to and from tables didn't disturb the oasis of tranquility that we sat in. Even the dogs lay flat, heads on front paws gazing around with interest at the changing scene. Jim's face had lost the worried intensity he'd worn now for days. I could tell he was still apprehensive, but the relaxation these few hours had afforded us could be seen most clearly in his face.

Not one of us wanted cake or dessert. "It's no good Maggie. They all look delicious and will taste great, but none of them will be as good as your baking. It's not worth us bothering," explained Martin. Then with an anxious look towards Maggie. "You have got some cakes and cookies for us back at the Priory?"

A roar of laughter arose from us all at the anxious question from Martin.

"Yes Martin, I baked yesterday. Cookies and lemon drizzle cake, two cakes. Our cake numbers seem to be growing." Maggie replied, casting a teasing look towards Gerald and Sam.

A text came in for Jim. He opened his phone and stared down at it. We all watched as he read it once. Then he took a deep breath, and read it again. Jim closed his phone and placed it with great care in his pocket, then he looked up and around the group. The silence deepened as he looked down at his hands, and then he took a deep breath and began to speak.

CHAPTER FORTY-TWO

We never knew what Jim's words were going to be. A tiny poodle with a pink bow in its topknot, glittering diamante collar, and to my amazement pink glittery nails danced up to our three dogs. Standing in front of our dogs, it broke into a series of noisy barks in their faces. Maisie rose to her feet and stared openmouthed at this dog. I could almost read the balloon comment above her head, and it wasn't complimentary! Her horrified glance towards Maggie was obviously saying, "is this dog for real?" Flora and Lottie were not standing for the insolence of this primped up dog. The cheek of it! Coming to bark in their faces when they were being so good, was appalling behaviour. Leaping to their feet they barked back. The café tables were spread out in the courtyard, a wall behind us, and the house in front of us. The barking grew louder, and the echoes when magnified made an incredible noise.

"We've finished, haven't we?" Jim jumped to his feet. He hated anything that drew attention to himself, and was extremely embarrassed by this doggy hullabaloo.

"Yes, let's go. The owner couldn't care less about her dog's behaviour. We'll leave." Maggie grabbed Maisie's lead, and she also jumped up from the table like Jim.

The woman unconcerned at the noise her dog had caused was in earnest conversation with two friends. A quick glance towards our table, and she called, "sweetie pops back to mummy, no barking poppet." Even the combined glares from all of us didn't seem to worry her.

***

Gathering our gift shop bags, and the dogs, we exited the

courtyard in a rush. But Sweetie Pops followed us, still barking. The men ran on ahead with the dogs, and as a buggy was getting ready to leave we helped Sheila up on it. As it was empty, we joined her and rode back to the car park. Sweetie Pops still barking, was finally left behind.

"Did you see the painted nails on that dog?" Sheila said in disgust. "Poor dog."

"Yes, but I don't know what to think about it. Maybe the dog likes being pampered and fussed over," I said.

"Nonsense! Most dogs enjoy puddles, and muddy patches of earth, and running through the grass, not worrying about their nail varnish getting chipped." Sheila's blunt reply made Maggie and I laugh.

"What was the text about?" Maggie whispered to me as the buggy drew closer to the gate and the men.

"I didn't see it, we'll have to wait until Jim feels like sharing it," I said.

"He looked stunned to me, and I'm certain he actually went pale," Sheila said.

"Nothing gets past Sheila does it?" I laughed and helped her down from the buggy.

The dogs greeted us as if we'd been away from them for weeks, not just a few moments. Sorting them out in the car ready for the journey home, we somehow gathered around Jim. Questioning looks were thrown in his direction, but not one of us dared ask.

Jim realised what we were doing, sighed, and leaned against the SUV. "You all want to know what was in the text I got. I realise that my reaction to it was obvious to you all." Nods of heads and murmurs of agreement followed that remark.

"Let's get back to the Priory and I'll explain everything. It's a long story, and a public car park is not the place for it."

***

Jim and I followed the SUV in my van. The dogs in the back of the SUV were looking back at the van. I waved at them, then became aware of Jim's chuckles beside me.

"Daisy you always defuse the situation somehow. If it's not words of wisdom, a sympathetic ear, you make me laugh. Do you really think the dogs appreciate you waving at them?"

"Yes I do. They know it's my van and we're in it. Waving to them is…" I couldn't finish that sentence, so I sat in dignified silence.

Jim chuckled again, and then turned towards me. His voice changed completely, and I could tell he was now in solemn serious mode.

"What was in the text? It alarmed you, didn't it?"

Jim clenched and unclenched his hands in his lap, and then stared straight down the road before answering me. "My friend, who is still active in the business, has discovered that my phone has been hacked."

"Now your phone. What about your computer? Has that also been hacked?"

"No, I don't think so. It doesn't matter anyway. All my notes and files are in the library on my PC in there. Other notes and files are printed out on my desk, or in a bookcase in the library. I don't work in the cottage, I haven't got the room, and the library has everything I need," Jim replied.

I knew Jim often worked late in the library. Sometimes I'd hear his footsteps across the courtyard. He'd enter his cottage and I could hear a faint click of the front door closing. Lottie and Flora would raise their heads listening to his footsteps, but they knew they were Jim's, and they would then fall asleep.

When we arrived and went into the Priory kitchen, Maggie had already cut slices of lemon drizzle cake, with a plate of chocolate chip cookies beside it. Mugs of coffee and tea were handed out and everybody began munching, but their attention was fixed firmly upon Jim. At the end of his story there were several comments, but it was Sheila who made us laugh. "No wonder you were such a grumpy Gus! All that Watching business and now your phone being hacked."

"Let's check your computer," said Martin. Everyone followed him into the library. Martin fiddled and clicked. "No, your computer is safe, but I think a few of these phishing emails you deleted may well have been attacks."

"Well, what about it? What are we going to do? The secret blackmailer and murderer and now the secret Watcher. I'm not sure I like this. I much preferred a bad person to follow and spy on, someone like Ferret Face," said Sheila.

"I've got to finish that bureau for a client. I've taken on so much stuff that I haven't got enough hours in the day." Sam stood up. "I'm not complaining! It's great and I'm enjoying it. Especially now Demelza does all the paperwork and invoices for us."

His words seem to be a signal. We all rose and left the library. There seemed little we could do, with either the Watcher, or the killer. And it was gnawing at us all. Every escapade that we had been embroiled in, we had initiated most of the action. This time we had to sit and wait…

***

The post van arrived next morning, and Harry called for

help. "Everyone knows that I come here each morning, and they give me parcels and letters with green ink. Help me carry this lot in. There's a lot of these parcels now, I expect a lot of folks are in a bit of a pickle. Still, I expect if they've got secrets that they're ashamed of, that's their lookout. Some people shouldn't behave the way they do. Serves them right, if they have to pay up to keep their secrets!"

Maggie gave Harry his usual cup of tea and cake, whilst we took the parcels through to the back kitchen to be dealt with. To our surprise, Harry didn't linger. He swallowed the tea, gobbled his cake, gave us all a curt nod and was gone. No usual chat. "Harry is behaving strangely. He's never been the same since he's been told to leave his cottage. It's understandable, but he's had other offers from local people. It's not as if he'll be homeless."

They smelt! Dead fish can smell bad, several days old dead fish smells really bad! There was a mad scramble through to the back kitchen with the smelly parcels. Matters grew more chaotic with the pets underfoot. We may have hated the aroma, but the dogs loved it! Even Cleo came running from my cottage to join in the fun.

"There were two parcels at the front door this morning, and now four more makes six," said Maggie. Wearing her usual kitchen gloves, myself with a borrowed pair, we spread them out in order. Or in as much order as possible, the written words above thc sad fish.

Jim put his phone in his pocket. "Tenby says to bring it all to the station, he's not got enough men to keep traipsing up here for a lot of dead fish."

"That's two haddock, a kipper fillet which smells the worst, and three mackerel. There's a label still stuck on one of the fish, it's Eric's fish label." Sheila said, waving it up in the air at us. It made the smell worse.

"Eric the fish man comes tomorrow morning," said Maggie.

"Let's follow him," said Sheila.

"We'd be noticed, stopping and starting after him," said Jim.

"Not if we knew where he stops and starts, and we had somebody at each local stop," Sheila said with a triumphant air.

"Sheila, that's a good idea. We could if only we had...," said Jim.

"I've got his dates and times for every local stop. Eric gives us one every so often, with the dates and times on it." Maggie reached into a kitchen drawer, lifted out the flyer and handed it to Jim. His excitement was obvious in his face, Sheila was bouncing up and down on her chair, the white curls bouncing about in rhythm. Both had come alive at the thought of action.

"I can't wait until tomorrow. I know that it will be a major turning point in our investigation, I can feel it in my bones!" Sheila prophesied as she stood on the doorway.

"Let's hope that prophecy comes true Sheila," Maggie said.

There was heartfelt agreement echoed by everyone when we left the kitchen to go to our homes.

CHAPTER FORTY-THREE

Lottie and Flora began growling and barking at the back door. Startled, I jumped to my feet staring as the door opened. After my pet's mealtime and their garden outing, I had locked the door when we came back in. But I hadn't drawn the bolt across, because I would be taking them out later before going to bed. A tall man stood in my kitchen, improbably dressed in a dark suit, white shirt and tie. The ski mask was an unusual touch. "Tell your dogs to be quiet. This is a tranquilizer gun; I don't want to use it on them or you." I bent down, and picked the dogs up, placing each one of them on the sofa, hushing them. I was terrified, yet puzzled by the intruder. He spoke in the most refined accent, and whilst terrified by his gun, I couldn't help noticing the sharp creases in his trousers, and the elegant cut of his suit. "Text your friend Jim to come here at once. A plain text giving him no clue as to my presence."

I picked up the phone, texted Jim and awaited his arrival. He had watched me write the text. There was no way I could warn Jim. He gestured with the gun. "Open the front door for him." I went to the front door, telling my dogs to stay. I was frightened he'd shoot them with that tranquilizer gun. I opened the door for Jim, and stepped back as he entered my cottage.

"Come in Jim. You and Daisy are going for a ride." Again he gestured with the gun, and we followed its signal to the back door.

Before following him, I patted my dogs, "Stay there, I'll be back shortly." They looked puzzled, but sat still on the sofa. I hoped and prayed that I would be back shortly.

"Who are you? What do you want with us?" Jim stood unmoving for a moment on the threshold of the back door, and stared at the man. He had recovered from the shock at seeing the intruder in my cottage. I could see Jim cataloguing the man's clothes, bearing and accent just as I had done. I wondered if he had come to any conclusion about this intruder. I knew I was at a loss, he was so far distant from the usual burglar type.

"We only wish to have a conversation with you. There is no need to be alarmed, we don't wish to hurt you. This is a tranquilizer gun. I have not felt the need to bring an actual gun, because I'm hoping that you will come along with me quietly with a minimum of fuss. I can assure you that you will be back safely after our conversation." The soft words spoken in that impeccable accent were meant to be reassuring. They were not.

The look that Jim gave me held warning, and I could tell he saw little option but to follow that man's instructions. I gave a last glance towards my pets, and went out the back door, following Jim, and conscious of the tall figure with the gun at my back.

***

"Down the lane, there's a car waiting for us." Set back from the lane, partly hidden by trees was the car. "Get in the back." I opened the door of the large gleaming black car and slid into the backseat, Jim following me. The man got into the passenger seat. The gun never left its focus on us. There was no way we could rush off, there was no way we could fight him. "Okay, drive." The man behind the wheel was also masked. His head was turned towards us, and I saw the glitter of his eyes as he looked at us. Then he drove off down the lane, away from the Priory.

Jim's hand reached for mine, and he gave me a reassuring squeeze. There was nothing either of us could do, so we sat back in the chauffeur driven car, and waited as we drove towards an unknown destination. All I could think of as we drove through the evening darkness was how luxurious this car was. Leather seats, and all the smart car accessories any keen motorist could wish for, meant that this was top of the range model. It puzzled me, as did our abductor. Well spoken, obviously a public-school accent, superbly dressed, with beautiful manners. Who was he? What did he want with us? Our previous escapades had been with villains that looked and sounded like villains!

The journey went on through back roads, across moorland, and seemed to take a long time. The car had a luxurious aroma, that smelled of leather upholstery, and lingering perfume of the most expensive kind, mingled with very faint traces of cigar smoke. Where were we going? What was being worked out for our arrival with these two men? My mind seemed to wander up and down trivial avenues. I realized that it must be a defense mechanism. The car began to slow down, and Jim gave my hand an urgent squeeze. He whispered to me. "Don't take any chances, let it play out, and see what they want from us."

"Okay," was my whispered reply. The drive we now entered was tree-lined with crunching gravel beneath the wheels of the car. We drew up in front of a large imposing stone-built mansion. It dominated the gardens which surrounded it.

"This way please," was the polite invitation spoken by our abductor, and he opened the car door for us. When we got out, he walked up to the front door, a huge oak carved monstrosity that swung open when he reached the top step. We followed the first man, the chauffeur close behind. Both Jim and I stood amazed at the marble expanse of the entry hall. Dotted around were statues, and bronzes, mostly life-size. "Yes, it's quite something, isn't it?" The first man had turned to look at our expressions as we gazed around. I presumed he smiled. It was difficult to see under that balaclava. "Down the corridor and turn left please."

***

We followed his instructions and walked into another astonishing room. It was a library with floor to ceiling bookshelves. The height of the bookshelves was catered for by two ladders on wheels. There were cozy nooks, each complete with desk and armchair, ideal for research, investigative studies, or complete absorption in a trashy novel. I was standing lost in this wonderland of books, until a nudge from Jim brought me back to my immediate surroundings and predicament. There was a large table in the centre of the library, around it sat five men and a woman. It looked bizarre in this place of learning that these five people should all be wearing balaclavas. The two vacant chairs at the head of the table were obviously for us. Our guide indicated them, and we walked forward and sat down.

I noted each person was expensively dressed. They were wearing casual clothes, but the expensive logos on T-shirts could not be missed. The woman wore a red silk dress of impeccable cut, and her watch was not a cheap one! I was fascinated by the unusual color on her nails, not pink, not purple, but an unusual depth of colour in between.

I said nothing. I waited. So did Jim. This situation was out of our control. We had done as our captors told us. Now we waited to hear the reason for our capture.

"I apologize for this unusual meeting. I do hope you were not inconvenienced." This was the opening gambit from the man facing us. Again I said nothing. Again Jim said nothing. I could sense the silence from both of us was unsettling the group before us. "You have realised we have been watching you Jim, and the work you have been doing."

Silence from both of us. It was the woman who spoke now, irritated by the whole business I could tell. "Let's get down to it, we know you are investigating the Knights Templars and the families around here. We now know that you are researching the lineage of these families with a view to finding deserted buildings, artefacts and lost burial places. What we want to know is what are you going to do with your findings?"

Jim finally spoke. "And you couldn't have come to my door and politely asked me that? You had to kidnap myself and Daisy, and bring us here for a discussion, with you all hidden behind your anonymity?"

The man spoke again. "Yes, we like to remain anonymous. We belong to a secret society that's been in existence for many years, if not centuries. It's safer that way. Over the generations we have safeguarded our heritage. We want to know what you intend to do with your research. We want to know if you are going to publish your findings."

"No! My research is purely for my own interest. There is no way that I would want publicity for myself, or for my research. I would intend if I found any objects or places of archaeological interest that I would then contact the relevant authorities, but it's doubtful any of my work would fall into that category." Jim's voice carried an intensity and honesty that I hoped would be apparent to our captors.

"And you? Daisy isn't it? What interest do you have in this research?" The woman asked, taking me by surprise. I was so interested in Jim's predicament that I hadn't taken account of my own. "I don't have any interest in it.

I sometimes accompanied Jim if he was going somewhere pleasant, where I could perhaps sketch or photograph."

The silence between these people was prolonged. Each one wrote on the slip of paper in front of them, and passed it down to the leader. The slips of paper were read, and placed one on top of the other. Jim was getting irritable at this long-winded display. Our abductor patted the slips of paper and finally spoke. "We are all agreed. It is unanimous that we don't think that you are a threat to our society. However, we would like your assurance, rather your promise to keep our secret and join our association. Both of you are welcome to become members." At the conclusion of his speech all balaclavas were removed, and the faces turned towards both of us were smiling. The woman in the scarlet dress fluffed up the blonde curls that had been squashed in the balaclava, and pulled a small compact from her handbag beside her chair to check her makeup.

I said nothing. Nor did Jim. We were both too astonished to speak. On the car ride I had feared for my life. I had wondered if I was going to end up buried on Bodmin moor, or hidden deep in a mine shaft. I know Jim must've felt the same. To be taken by gunpoint against your will, and then to have this crowd smiling at you as if it was a pleasant drinks party, was both unbelievable and annoying!

It was Jim who rallied first. "What association?"

"Did you recognize the sign on the stone we left in your lounge?"

"Yes, it was the Hooked X," Jim replied.

"We are a group who have grown up searching for elusive artifacts hidden in Cornwall by the descendants of the Knights Templar families. As you know the Hooked X can be found on stones and documents relating to the

Knights Templars. It can be seen throughout Europe, in Christopher Columbus's signature, and even on rune stones in America. We don't want anyone to know what we are doing, or our identities. That is why we had you under surveillance, so we could be certain you were the right person to join us. Your research already may be valuable to us. Added to our own research, it could be instrumental in finding previously hidden domiciles and artefacts of the Knights Templars."

**

It must've been two hours later when we walked into my cottage. The log burner was still on, but burning low. Our return was welcomed by my pets, who were not distressed at our abrupt removal, but rather to my annoyance had obviously slept throughout our absence. Without a word to each other we entered my kitchen area. I put the kettle on, and got my mug ready with a teabag. Jim opened the cupboard got out a glass and the whisky. Taking both he sat down in the chair beside the log burner. Leaning forward he opened its door and threw a log on to it. The flames licked round the log, and it seemed to glow with an intensity that brought a new life into the room.

"So we are now members of the society of the Hooked X," I murmured as I sat down in the opposite chair with my mug of tea. I lifted it as if toasting Jim, before finally drinking it. "Congratulations Jim, is that the right thing to say to you? Are you delighted to become a member?"

"I don't know what to think. That feeling of dread, of being watched is obviously over now. I expect the cameras will be taken away, and that life will go back to normal. Why the hell they couldn't just have knocked at my door, and asked me outright, instead of all this cloak and dagger stuff I'll never know." The glass of whisky was emptied and set down sharply onto the little table.

"They seemed a very polite, if rather odd bunch. What about Gerald? How will you keep him from knowing about them? They obviously didn't think he had much to offer them, or they would've included him in the abduction. Why me? Why was I included?"

"I expect it was because you've always been involved with my investigations, especially the one at Temple," Jim replied.

"What will you tell your spy friends?"

"Daisy, I just don't know what to think. Do you mind? I need to go and think this all through quietly, and get to bed. I feel shattered by it." Jim rose to his feet with a quick movement, and he had almost reached the door before he turned back, lent over me and with one finger raised my chin, gave me a quick kiss before leaving.

The door had been closed behind him for several minutes. "Goodnight Jim, sleep well." I said and drank my tea, sorted out my pets and went to bed myself.

CHAPTER FORTY-FOUR

Eric the fish man had five stops around the village, and just outside it. After discussion, we picked the four most likely spots at which our blackmailer could buy his fish. It was arranged we would split up, and hang about each stop at the time Eric was expected. The central stop beside the village community shop seemed the most unlikely spot for our blackmailer to buy his fish. So Sheila sitting on her mobility scooter was given that one. Her excitement at this task had her curls bouncing around her. Her large bag was filled with necessities, including Mace, a whistle, and a small wooden truncheon. The second one outside the pub was given to Martin and Gerald, as again we thought that an unlikely one. Martin being so nervous, he wouldn't know what to do if Eric did have the blackmailer in front of him. Jim and Maggie had the one leading to Bodmin. The one furthest out the village leading up to the moor was given over to Sam and myself.

"I think it likely he will buy at one of the two stops leading out of the village. Text me if you spot one of our suspects. Don't do anything. Watch, take photos and check out with Eric what they buy from him," Jim said, and checked his watch yet again. "It's time to get ready. Try to keep out of sight if at all possible."

"Do you really think it will be Francesca, Annie or Leah?" Maggie asked as she shrugged on her jacket.

"They seem the most likely, Annie has those potions and herbs at her cottage, Leah is her surly daughter, and Francesca has the Italian father. They all have the knowledge about the Mafia and the dead fish. Francesca is desperate for money to get to Exeter. Leah copies Francesca in everything, and is keen to get money to keep up with her cousin. As for Annie, she seems a very complex person, and I wouldn't know why she would do it, but she is a likely suspect nevertheless."

"I know Annie, I've known her for many years, admittedly she can be a bit strange, but I don't think there is any bad in her. Whoever has been doing this is evil," said Maggie. "Money is behind the blackmailing scheme. But these malicious attacks on favorite pets, plants and objects throughout the village is spiteful and malicious. I don't think any of the three of them has got an evil streak like that in them," she added, winding her scarf around her neck.

"When Eric the fish van has done his rounds, we may find out exactly who it is. Let's go and find ourselves a blackmailer and a killer," said Jim.

"Are you sure you want to do it Daisy? It's not too dangerous?" Maggie looked at me as I put on the helmet Sam had given to me. I knew she was thinking 'at my age,' but at least she had the good sense not to say it out loud.

"Sam promised he'd go slow, and it's only just up the hill. Look at it this way Maggie, I'm in my seventies, I've never ridden pillion on the back of a motorbike before. It's something else to cross off my bucket list."

I was scared. I smiled and gave a jaunty wave to the others. I was not going to let anyone see how scared I actually was. The noise and vibration of the motorcycle had me shaking, and I had to swallow hard in case my breakfast came up. Once we got going and I finally opened my eyes it wasn't too bad. I was just beginning to enjoy it when Sam drew into the side of the road.

"Up ahead, see that driveway. Eric parks his fish van up there; the owners have given him permission. If I wheel the bike into this field opening, we can wait here. I don't think we'll be noticed this far away from the van.

But we can see clearly who's going to park there."

The text came in from Jim, *Eric says Harry has been buying loads of fish at your stop.* A few moments later, *we are on our way to join you...* Eric would be coming to us next, before going to Bodmin.

"Here's the fish van!" Sam shouted and the van drove past us towards the drive opening.

I could feel my whole body stiffen, and I squinted around Sam to watch. Eric got out and began opening his van up. A lady on a bicycle rode up, bought some fish, had a chat with Eric, put the fish in her basket and rode off. A black car came, and an elderly man got out, took a ready wrapped parcel from Eric, paid him and drove off. We could hear snippets of conversation drift down towards us. Just as we thought our time was being wasted, a car drove up. Unwashed, in a dreadful condition, it jolted to a stop. A man got out and walked over to the fish van.

"It's Harry! Get off the bike Daisy, I'll block his car in."

"Hello Harry, back again? That's a lot of fish that you are getting through these days. You never shopped with me before, must like it a lot now. Bargain offers? Yes, what about this lot?" Eric had a loud voice which drifted back down the hill towards us.

"Okay but…" My words were drowned out when Sam powered up the bike, and raced towards the fish van and Harry.

Like slow-motion I saw Harry turn around with his arms full of fish and stare at Sam on the motorbike.

"Hey Harry, I want a word with you," Sam shouted as he drew up beside Harry.

The older man's eyes widened as he looked at Sam, and then at me running up behind Sam. Harry began to run to his car. Sam revved up the motorbike and followed him. Eric stood open mouthed beside his van, wondering what was going on. It was Harry that made the first move. After a few steps he opened out his parcel of fish. "You won't catch me," he shouted at Sam and threw a large cod fillet at the motor bike. He followed that with a couple of kippers.

It was disastrous. Sam's front wheel ran over and squished the fish. The skin and scales of the fish seemed to explode into the air, and became tangled in the wheel. The wheel lost purchase on the road and slid along the tarmac. Harry grabbed a slippery trout, and threw it at the bike. It flew into the air, and hit the second wheel which began to slide in yet another direction. Sam fought valiantly trying to hold onto the bike and ward off the fishy attacks. It was a losing battle, and the bike slid sideways, and Sam flew off onto the road. Harry threw his last fish, which was a very large mackerel. Sam was struggling to his feet, but they kept slipping on the fishy mush which was splattered across the road. It hit Sam full in the face "That stopped you and your precious motorbike!" Harry gave an evil laugh, then ran for his car.

I had reached the fish van. Grabbing a huge mackerel by the tail I threw it at Harry's back. It hit him on the head, and he lurched forward. It didn't stop him. Sam was still struggling to his feet, the slimy fish halting his progress. Harry turned back to grin at me. He'd reached his car and opened the door. He thought he was safe, ready for his escape.

I dithered. Yes, I know it's my usual fault. But all the large fish had gone. Harry must have bought them. There was the fisherman's knife. No, that was too dangerous for me! I didn't want to spend my last years in a jail cell if I accidently killed Harry. There was only the seafood left. A lobster and a few crabs. The lobster was big, it's dark shell shiny. And those claws! Held in place by rubber bands, they were moving ceaselessly and angrily. Swallowing hard, gingerly, I grasped its middle. I cringed when the legs and claws waved frantically at my touch.

I threw it at Harry. The lobster didn't like flying through the air, it reacted violently. One of the rubber bands snapped and pinged, and flew off. The lobsters initial contact with something, anything, after its flight, caused it to grip that first thing with force. It just so happened to be Harry's ear! Harry sank to the ground shouting and screaming. That lobster had hit him full in the face, its claws catching his hair and ears.

"Great shot!" Shouted Eric, and threw a couple of crabs at Harry. Harry now had his hands and face covered in scratches from the crustaceans.

Sam reached him, and Eric and I joined him, looking down at the defeated Harry. The crabs, and the lobster were still moving, and crawling all over him.

"Harry! It was you that sent those blackmailing letters! That's why you've been buying this fish. Why? Why did you do it?" I shouted out as I reached him. I couldn't comprehend the fact that the kindly older postman was in fact not only an evil blackmailer, but possibly the killer. "Why Harry?"

Holding onto the car door, he turned towards me. The kindly face of Harry I'd known for some time disappeared. His face contorted into a sly evil glare. "I needed the money. Going to be turned out of my cottage. Needed the money to buy it. Took it from those that had it, and had plenty to spare."

"Why damage things that people loved? Why kill Luke and Roy? And why did you try and kill my pets?" I was staring at him now.

"I had nothing! Why should anyone else have anything. That Roy deserved it, and that stupid Hilda tried to threaten me. Luke saw me with the green ink and tried to blackmail me. As for you, and those stupid animals…"

A car drew up with a squeal of brakes. "It was Harry. All this time it was Harry. He confessed," I shouted to Jim and Maggie as they ran towards us.

"That he did, I heard every word of it. I'll swear to it in any court of law. Harry confessed to all them evil things that have been happening in the village," Eric the fish man said, shaking his head.

"You certainly stopped him Daisy," Sam said. He was wiping down his jacket and trousers, trying to get the scales and slime off them. "A lobster! Yet another unusual weapon!"

Harry rose to his feet, brushing the last crab from his jacket. It had been clinging to his pocket and seemed unwilling to let go. Now he had been caught he seemed intent on telling us all why he had done it. In a bizarre way he was trying to justify himself.

"Lived in my cottage for seventeen years, tended that garden until it became a thing of beauty, and it was so productive. Looking forward to my retirement, and what happens? I've got to get out! The owner decides to put up the rent knowing I can't afford it. Why? So that he can do it up, and have it as a holiday let. Or I can buy it! At an inflated price! Everyone else has things they love. They have money as well. So thought I'd get myself some. I discovered Roy blackmailing, so thought I could join in with him. He wasn't going to have that, he wanted it all for himself. And how he argued with me, sneered at me. He's not laughing now. That Hilda, she knew I'd argued with Roy, she guessed it was me that did for him. Thought I'd shut her mouth, even tried to get her in the hospital."

There was no stopping him. Not that we tried. He just

stood there, justifying himself. He thought that we were in the wrong, and what he had done was quite reasonable.

"As for you," Harry pointed towards me, and Sam. "Spending good money on those silly animals, and you with that stupid bike. All of you spending money whilst I haven't got enough to buy my place. That was my cottage, he might've owned it, but it was me that made it as it is, beautiful inside and out. He had no right to sell it. No right! No right!"

Tenby drew up with a couple of policemen who quickly took Harry away in the car.

"He's confessing? To everything? Both murders? And all the other incidents and all the blackmailing?" Tenby was stunned. He kept shaking his head. "Confessing to everything, never heard of that before. Confessing to everything."

"What made you think of this fish van business? And who was it captured him?"

Eric who had been putting away his fish, ready for his next stop, took it upon himself to explain everything. He was enjoying himself. "It was her! She rushed up after the guy on the motorcycle crashed. Harry threw the fish at him, right onto his bike wheels. Poor chap never stood a chance, the wheels slid every which way, and he took a tumble. She came up to him, and she chucked a lobster at him. Then I chucked a couple of crabs at him. He didn't like them! Knocked him sideways. That Harry just fell down there, and started confessing," Eric told the policeman.

"A lobster? And crabs!" Tenby just sniffed, stared at me for a long moment, nodded and walked back to the car.

***

That night was spent in a celebration. There was a lessening of fear, and the dread of something horrible going to happen. Sheila of course, was in full swing, laughing and joking and trying to dance with Martin when he put some music on. A unanimous decision had been the rescue of the lobster and the crabs. They were placed with great ceremony back in the sea.

I went into the kitchen. It felt unreal that the horrible trauma was now over. The sense of unknown assailants had left me jittery. I couldn't get my head around the fact that it had been Harry all along. My image of Harry was him sitting smiling at our kitchen table. His great love of Maggie's coffeecake was all I could connect with him, not an evil murdering blackmailer. The kettle had boiled, and I reached for a mug. I popped in the teabag. The others were still laughing and chatting in the library. I made my tea, and stood at the Priory kitchen window staring out into the night across the courtyard. It was over. Yet another adventure on Bodmin Moor had ended with the capture of a man not one of us had suspected. His friendship with Francesca's Italian father, had been unknown to us. Would that have made a difference? I'm not sure that it would. Harry did not look like a villain; he didn't act like a villain. I still found unbelievable that he could've done…

"Daisy? You all right?" Jim had joined me in the kitchen. I nodded at him and sighed.

"How did we get it so wrong?"

"Nothing has been straightforward in this situation. Remember we were trying to cope with the Watcher as well. But I do admit, I never, ever would've suspected Harry," said Jim.

An incoming text from Violet alerted me. *"Daisy, I've got a message from someone who says he is our brother. He wants to meet up with us tomorrow morning."*

Coming soon Daisy and the Daffodils of Death.
The next book with Daisy and her friends in yet more
hilarious escapades!

About The Author

Scottish born, I now live on the Jurassic Coast of Dorset with my husband, and Monty our enormous cavalier. Our two adult children live in N. Yorkshire and Zurich Switzerland.

Changing primary schools, five in total, meant that I was unable to read until given special lessons. This gave me a deep love of reading, and being an only child, I devoured books. Following this experience, I became a teacher. Unable to continue because of mobility problems, due to E.D.S., I became a home tutor. After extra training, I specialised in children with reading difficulties.

I studied botanical art for many years but developed RSI. Determined to carry on with my art and writing, I now paint with my left hand and dictate all my novels. I still paint flowers trying to capture their fleeting beauty.

An avid reader, I love cosy mysteries, where the murder doesn't scare me to death! I enjoy writing humorous mysteries, with eccentric characters, who always get in a pickle! Many of my books are set in Cornwall which holds a special place in my heart.

Find me on Facebook, Instagram, Pinterest and Twitter and on my website.

www.janeyclarke.com

www.blossomspringpublishing.com

Printed in Great Britain
by Amazon

17875656R00140